FOUR THINGS MY GEEKY-JOCK-OF-A-BEST-FRIEND MUST DO IN EUROPE

by

Jane Harrington

DARBY CREEK PUBLISHING

To Dad & Mom—
my traveling buddies through Ireland, Williamsburg, and life.

This version was edited for content for Scholastic Book Fairs.

Cataloging-in-Publication

Text copyright © 2006 by Jane Harrington Shapiro
Cover photography by John Sanderson copyright © 2006 by Darby Creek Publishing
Cover design by John Margeson
Layout by Kelly Rabideau

Harrington, Jane.
Four things my geeky-jock-of-a-best-friend must do in Europe / by Jane Harrington.
        p. ; cm.
ISBN-13: 978-1-58196-041-9 Library bound edition
ISBN-10: 1-58196-041-7 Library bound edition
ISBN: 1-58196-047-6 Scholastic Book Fairs edition softcover
Summary: Written in the form of letters to her best friend, Delia, back home, Brady tells of her
adventures while on a Mediterranean cruise with her mother and of her progress on Delia's list of
things she must do, including the search for a "code-red Euro-hottie."
1. Self-confidence—Juvenile fiction. 2. Teenage girls—Juvenile fiction. 3. Friendship—Juvenile
fiction. 4. Mothers and daughters—Juvenile fiction. [1. Self-confidence—Fiction. 2. Teenage
girls—Fiction. 3. Friendship—Fiction. 4. Mothers and daughters—Fiction.] I. Title. II. Author.
PZ7.H23815 Fo 2006
[Fic] dc22
OCLC: 60636984

DARBY CREEK PUBLISHING

Published by Darby Creek Publishing
7858 Industrial Parkway
Plain City, OH 43064
www.darbycreekpublishing.com

Printed in the United States of America

1 2 3 4 5 6 7 8 9 10

Dear Delia,

It is the first day of my trip.

Hm. I guess if you're reading this, then it can't be the first day anymore. Considering how slow the mail is, I may even be home.

But how can I be home? It's the first day of my trip.

How sad. I've already confused myself. Of course, it's not my fault—it's YOUR fault. I'm just following the first of your (rather bossy) instructions, which you (rather rudely) wrote on my hand, under the title:

3

FOUR THINGS
MY GEEKY-JOCK-OF-A-
BEST-FRIEND
<u>MUST</u> <u>DO</u>
IN EUROPE

Nice, Delia. REAL nice. I love you, too.

You know, a person isn't a GEEK just because she gets better grades than a certain OTHER person. AND a person isn't a JOCK just because she does a lot of sports. (Well, okay, maybe she IS a jock if she does a lot of sports, but WHATEVER.)

It IS an HONOR, though, Delia, to have your creative work—in PERMANENT MARKER—all over the palm of my hand, on my fingers, and extending up my wrist. It is just GREAT! (NON. That's Italian for "not.") Your tiny printing and artsy squiggles bring to mind that cool henna painting women do on their hands when they get married in India. Only I'm not getting married, I'm not in India, and it's not particularly cool. And I'm fairly certain the Indian henna painters don't write out lists of things to do. Such as:

#1: WRITE REAL LETTERS TO YOUR
BEST FRIEND EVERY DAY, DESCRIBING
THRILLING ADVENTURES.

So, okay, I'm writing to you, but—unfortunately—I have no thrilling adventures to tell you about. We are still at the airport, where we've been sitting for hours. We had to get here real early for "security checks," which turned out to be a lot of real intensive, highly invasive, totally scary NOTHING. We've just been sitting here and sitting here, bored, surrounded by all the other people who got here early, and no one is checking anything—except maybe their watches.

My mother (or "mio madre" in Italian, pronounced mee-o mah-drah, according to our phrase book) keeps trying to show me pictures of Italian sculpture in this book she's got, but I feel it is my obligation—as a new member of the World Teen Corps—to appear bored by things like that. Having this letter to write is a good excuse for not paying attention to her, since I don't want to be rude about it. Of course, given what I discovered this morning, I think I have good REASON to be rude.

It all began when she told me to put "essentials" in my carry-on pack for the plane ride. "In case the luggage is lost," she said, "we should have things to get us through several nights." I thought "several nights" of stuff was a bit much, but I decided not to question it, since she's been sort of nervous lately and acting a little weird(er than usual). I know it's all because

5

this is her first trip to Europe, but she's making ME nervous, too, since, OF COURSE, it's my first time, too. It's amazing that she's gotten to be forty (or however old she is) without EVER going outside the U.S. She grew up in one of those ginormous families, and she says even a trip to McDonald's was a major outing that had to be planned and saved up for weeks in advance.

ANYWAY . . . I scrounged my room for "essentials" and began stuffing them in my pack—you know: CD player and CDs, chocolate, sunglasses, gum, lip gloss, more chocolate, lollipops, magazine, etc. At some point, while doing this, it occurred to me that I'd forgotten to get a new book for the trip. So, I decided to search the house for a paperback I hadn't read. That's when I stumbled across this old, dilapidated book on a shelf in the living room, entitled: <u>2500 First Names of Boys and Girls with Their Origins, Meanings, Etc., Etc.</u>

Intrigued, I started looking through it, and I found some of the most FABULOUS names—Prunella, Urania, Dorcas, Hagar, Portia, Sela, stuff like that. And the meanings were even better. Sela, for instance, means "a rock," and Portia means "pig woman." (Oh yeah, I'll be naming my kid THAT.) I was having a great old time, laughing out loud at the thought of kids in the halls at school calling out, "HEY, DORCAS! DON'T FORGET ABOUT VOLLEYBALL PRACTICE TONIGHT!" when I got the idea to look up my OWN name. At which point I stopped laughing, shut the book, and went searching for someone who had some serious explaining to do: mio madre.

I figured she was in her bedroom packing, but it turns out she was in the dining room dropping her snake into a pillowcase. This did not strike me as odd (we're talking about my mother here), but it did strike me as funny. Even though I knew perfectly well that she was putting it in the pillowcase so it wouldn't get loose while she cleaned the tank (something which has been known to happen), I couldn't resist saying, "Oh, so THAT'S what you meant by 'essentials.'"

She laughed, and I was thinking how nice it was that she appreciated my sense of humor, until I remembered that she was in big trouble. I held up the name book, and she immediately volunteered, enthusiastically, that she'd used it to pick all our names.

"So, then, you read the meanings," I said, leafing through the pages, stopping at my little sister's name. "And Clare means 'the light.'"

My mother smiled and nodded as she set the pillowcase on the floor.

I skipped forward a few pages, until I found Irene's name. "Oh, this is a beauty," I said. "My older sister's name means 'peaceful.'"

Mom hesitated a sec, then nodded as she reached into the tank for the water dish.

"But this is, by far, the best one," I said, finding—after an appropriately dramatic delay—the entry for my own name. "I'll read the whole meaning: 'Brady, male or female, from the Gaelic "Bradach," meaning "broad clearing"—or "the big one."'"

(I'm guessing, at this point in my letter, Delia, that you are having a hysterical laughing fit. To this, I have one thing to say: Happy Bunny says ZIP IT!)

"Huh," Mom said in an isn't-that-interesting sort of way. Refilling the water dish and returning it to the tank, she added, "Finished packing yet?"

(Typical mother move. When in trouble, nag.)

Choosing to ignore such a completely ridiculous and totally irrelevant question, I asked her, "Is it possible to be a dyslexic clairvoyant?"

"I don't know," she said, chuckling. "Why?"

"You picked names that were an absolute backward prediction of my sisters' personalities."

"Huh," she said again, as she reached into the tank and scooped out the old litter.

"Mom," I said, "HOW could you give Clare—CLARE, who is in OUTER SPACE—a name that means 'the light'? And Irene—well, I won't even go there."

"If I have this dyslexic power to predict the future . . . backwards," my mother said over her shoulder, as she dumped fresh litter into the tank, "then you won't ever be 'the big one,' right?"

(I ask you: Do all parentals have this annoying habit of using LOGIC to twist arguments to their advantage?)

"Unfortunately," I sighed, "I already AM 'the big one.' Haven't you noticed? I'm huge." To this—the honest, humiliating admission of this growing (SHUT UP, DELIA) problem in my life, my mother: LAUGHED. So I: Stuck my tongue out at her. (Immature, I agree, but it was an involuntary reaction—completely out of my control.)

"Well, THAT was inappropriate, Brady," she said. (EVERYTHING is inappropriate these days. Movies, songs,

TV shows, apparently my tongue—I can't keep up.) "You're not huge," she continued. "You have an athletic build."

"Isn't 'athletic build' just a euphemism for BIG?" I asked.

Ignoring me (probably intimidated by my use of advanced vocabulary), she reached down to pick up the pillowcase.

"Tell me, Mom, HONESTLY," I said, "do you think the way I've been growing lately is, uh, NORMAL?"

"NO!" she cried.

Shocked by such a bold display of honesty—from an adult, at least—I gave her an outraged-teenagy sort of glare. (I've been working on that.)

"I didn't mean NO about THAT—I meant NO about THIS," she said, holding up the pillowcase, which was quite obviously empty. Poking her finger through a hole in the seam, she added, "Longfellow's loose."

Then the house filled with a sound akin to an elephant stampeding down the stairs, which—as you've probably guessed—was my dear older sister.

"Irene, 'the peaceful one,' has awakened," I announced.

"Distract her, PLEASE," my mother said, dropping to the floor.

Though it was hard not to feel sorry for her there, pathetically prowling around on all fours, it was not a sense of sympathy which prompted me to help my mother. It was merely the desire to ward off one of my sister's tizzie fits, which she is known to have about, well, EVERYTHING, as you—and all other people with ears—are aware.

I stood in the doorway and cheerfully said, "Hi!" as my sister stomped down the last of the stairs.

"What's wrong with you?" Irene asked. "Why are you being so nice? And why are you standing in the doorway?"

"No reason," I said, still smiling.

She stared at me a second and then said, "When did you get so BIG?"

"MOM! I yelled, turning to look at my mother, who was now under the dining room table. "I TOLD you I'm big!"

"She just means you're taller than she is, dear," my mother said.

But Irene, in her 'peaceful' way, said, "NO, I mean she's BIGGER than I am. And I DON'T like it. I'm three years older than she is, so why did SHE end up with BIGGER—" She stopped suddenly at that point, apparently taking notice of the fact that our mother was slithering around on the floor. "What are you looking for?" Irene asked.

"Oh, nothing important!" Mom said perkily.

"Uh, why did I end up with bigger what?" I asked Irene.

"Don't tell me, DON'T TELL ME!" Irene yelled, ignoring me, and getting her tizz all revved up. "You are NOT planning to leave on a trip with that SNAKE loose, Mom! NO WAY!"

"Dad will be here," my mother said, her head halfway under the radiator, "and Clare. They'll find it if—"

"Oh, no! No! NO!" Irene shrieked. "This ISN'T going to happen. You're going to FIND the snake, Mom. Why do we have a snake in the FIRST place? NORMAL FAMILIES DON'T HAVE SNAKES!"

Even though I wanted to get to the bottom (or top, I suspected) of what Irene almost said, I knew there was no getting through to her for a while. So, I went upstairs to finish packing.

As I passed my little sister's room, I noticed she was on the computer (per usual). I decided to stop and ask her something.

"Clare," I said, "do I look bigger to you?"

"Bigger than what?" she asked, staring at the screen, which had about twenty-five IM boxes stacked up all over it and a whole pack of virtual ferrets crawling around.

"Bigger than I was before," I said.

"Before what?" she asked, still tapping away on the keyboard.

Reminding myself that Clare isn't really in the same time-space continuum as the rest of us, I headed to my own room to see if I still fit through the door.

WHEN did my life get so humiliating? Oh, yeah! It was yesterday. At the mall. With you! Which brings me to the second (really pushy) instruction you wrote on my hand:

#2: WEAR THE BIKINI . . .

I can't BELIEVE I let you force me to buy that thing. All I wanted was a nice, one-piece, racing-style swimsuit, like my old one, which seems to have SHRUNK or something—stop laughing—but NOOOO. You had to go on and on about how people don't wear one-piece, racing-style suits on Mediterranean cruises. How people ONLY wear bikinis.

HOW EMBARRASSING that I had to get different sizes. I don't mind so much that the bottoms are a medium. It's the top that bugs me—I can't BELIEVE I needed the big one. (I said, STOP laughing.)

Still, I wouldn't have such a problem actually WEARING the thing—it's blue, after all, and you know how I feel about blue—if it weren't for your next (outrageously pushy) instruction:

#3: IN PUBLIC!!!

Oy vey. (As my grandmother says.)

You think this is no big deal. You tell me, "I've been wearing bikinis since I was ten!" No offense, Delia, but I don't think you're a whole lot bigger now than you were at ten. But me? It's like I've been exposed to radiation. If you had THAT going on, you might be self-conscious about wearing a bikini, too.

(Well, maybe.)

Sorry, Delia, but I'll have to finish this rant later. We're BOARDING! YES!

Your globally active friend,

Brady

Dear Delia,

It's a whole two hours since the last letter, and I wish I could at least report that we are flying over the Atlantic Ocean, but the truth is, we still haven't left the DC airport. Yes, we did board, and yes, it was on time, and, yes, we even rolled down the runway, but then we had to stop because of a major thunderstorm in Chicago, which is where we're supposed to get our flight to Rome. So we're sitting here on the runway. Well, we're not sitting on the runway. We're in seats, in the plane. On the runway.

You may be wondering WHY we're flying to Chicago at all. Of course, this is assuming you have some knowledge of geography, which is unlikely, since you hate that subject. So, I'll explain all this at a level appropriate to your understanding—say, first grade? It's like this: Our airport is in Washington, DC. (With me so far?) Chicago is WEST of DC, while Rome is EAST of DC. WEST and EAST are OPPOSITE directions. So, NOW, of course, you are thinking, "WHY would they fly in the direction that is AWAY from the place they are going?"

That's a very good question, Delia! But I'm not going to tell you the answer. It has to do with airlines and hubs and cruise packages and it's all MUCH too boring to talk about. I know this for a fact, because my mother talked about it for an hour. Finally, I had to resort to the only proven method for distracting her: Georgia Nicholson. I rooted through my pack until I found a copy of <u>Away Laughing on a Fast Camel</u>, which I opened and began reading. She forgot completely about her hub-and-cruise-package jag, and we went right into the same conversation we always have when she sees me reading (or re-reading) (or re-re-reading) a Georgia book. It went like this:

MY MOTHER: Those books are so inappropriate.

ME: But, Mom, you've never read one. Aren't you judging a book by its cover?

MY MOTHER: Yes, you're right. Let me borrow one, and I'll read it.

ME: No!

Then she left me alone—as she always does—and I immersed myself in Georgia's painfully familiar but nonetheless extremely humorous problems. It wasn't as fun as reading out loud with you, late at night, in British accents, but it did pass the time, and bloody well. (Why do the Brits use the word "bloody" all the time? Ew.)

Speaking of Britishness, that was fun watching <u>Bridget Jones's Diary</u> the other day. Except when my mother came home and had that fit about us watching an "inappropriate" movie. What I want to know is, IF she thought that movie was SO inappropriate then WHY did she leave it IN the DVD player when she left for work? And, if it's SO inappropriate why did I hear her laughing hysterically when SHE was watching it the night before? Really, what kind of mother is THAT?

I'm wondering something. Are all parents as totally weird as mine? I mean, take the idea for this trip, for instance. Every other Catholic-Jewish (or Cashewish, as YOU say) kid I know has a confirmation, a bar mitzvah, or a bat mitzvah, because their parents do the, uh, normal thing and pick a religion. But my parents? They invent, for their daughters, the "not mitzvah," an "educational coming-of-age trip." Don't get me wrong—I'm NOT complaining. I'm sure a trip to Europe is a whole lot more fun than CCD or Hebrew school, and I'm REALLY glad we saved up all this money so I could do it. I'm lucky, too, that they didn't change their minds about the whole thing, which they almost did after Irene's trip to Greece with my dad, when she called home every day, screaming (very expensively) about how she threw up all over a hydrofoil, and how they almost had to spend the night on the streets of Athens because their reservations got screwed up, and how a car suddenly appeared on the sidewalk and almost ran her over, and yadayada. It's just that the thought of being away with only my mother is a little scary. I'm used to buffers—television, computer, music, telephone, dad, sisters, the snake.

My mother says there will be lots of teenagers on the cruise ship, but how will I ever get up the courage to introduce myself to strangers without you there to make me do it? As we both know, Delia, YOU are the social one. SO, the thought of being around a whole bunch of new people without my best friend is

FRIGHTENING. You HAD to have KNOWN this, so WHY are you torturing me with this last (EXTREMELY BOSSY) order:

#4: MEET A CODE-RED EURO-HOTTIE.

WHY would I EVER agree to this?

Hm. I think the question is, actually: Why DID I ever agree to this?

Better question: How do I DO it?

I know, I know. You told me a million times. (How can I forget? I had to wrestle you to the ground to keep you from writing the instructions on my leg.) You meet a guy that's Euro—that is, from Europe—and then you rate his level of hottiness on a color-coded scale. Sort of like the ozone and terrorism warning systems, only red means GOOD when it comes to a hottie, and not that you should stop breathing air or move into your basement.

Simple. Except for that "meet a guy" part. How do I do THAT? I think you have to be, well, sort of, uh, YOU to pull this off.

You know how Ms. Heath went on and on (and on) in Human Growth about those "raging teenage hormones" that change the balance of chemicals in our brains and make us feel different? (Which, by the way, is pretty much what is happening in a mentally ill person's brain.) Well, I think that's your problem. Not that you're mental, but that you're DIFFERENT lately. You are (and don't take this the wrong way, or anything) OBSESSED with the opposite sex. That's why it would be easier for YOU to find these Euro-hotties.

It's NOT that I'm afraid of BOYS, Delia. I've played baseball since I was five, you know, and my teammates have ALWAYS been boys. Of course, we don't TALK. And I'm not entirely sure they have even figured out I'm a girl, but whatever.

I know, I know, you keep telling me it will be EASY. That Euro-hotties will be everywhere in the Mediterranean. EVERY-WHERE, you say. But I'm wondering something, Delia. How do YOU know so much about the Mediterranean? Have you ever BEEN to the Mediterranean? Huh? HUH?

I'm arguing with you, and you're not even here.

SAD. Molto (that's Italian for "very") sad.

Brady

Friday night, or maybe early
Saturday morning, over the Atlantic Ocean
(I'm thinking Bermuda Triangle)

Dear Delia,

I've been inside airplanes for so many hours I have lost my grip on reality. You're probably thinking that you can't lose something you never had, and my answer to that is: Go away. Oh yeah, you're already away. I mean, I'M away. OBVIOUSLY, I'm going stir crazy in this seat. Earlier, I had this incredible urge to do laps of high-knees in the aisles. (I know you think that's a double funny—the way people look running with their knees going up in the air AND the way "high-knees" sounds—but that's because you're very immature). Unfortunately, high-knees are something you definitely have to do with a group of people, so I just walked up and down the aisle instead. After a while, though, the flight attendants appeared with the food and drink carts, which made me feel frighteningly like Ms. Pacman. So I had to sit back down.

We are on the way to Rome now, which I should be glad about since we almost missed the plane. Or I should say we THOUGHT we almost missed it, the WHOLE time we were running in the Chicago airport, which is about as big as the entire city of DC, I'm pretty sure, AND as crowded. We were really, really late getting to Chicago on account of the storm, but Mom kept telling me (over and over, even though I never expressed any concern, whatsoever) that the flight to Rome HAD to be delayed because ALL the flights were delayed, etc., etc. But when we FINALLY got to Chicago and saw the monitors in the airport, we discovered that the Rome flight was SOMEHOW, by some MIRACLE, on time, which I figured had to do with the Pope, since he lives in Rome. (Which I took as a sign that maybe I should consider

Catholicism for a religious pastime.) We were at Gate 400, I think, and we needed to get to Gate 3, so we ran and ran and ran and got to the gate JUST IN TIME for the digi-sign over the counter to flash with the message: FLIGHT 70 TO ROME DELAYED. (So I lost interest in Catholicism. Oh well.)

I collapsed on the floor in a heap of human tiredness, and my mother—in an absurdly optimistic way—said, "Well, we're getting there, aren't we?" To which I replied, "Mom (gasp, gasp), we're further from Rome than we were when we started the trip this morning." She responded to this by saying, "Do you have to be so contrary?" And I responded to that by saying, "Yes, actually," and I went on to tell her about the chemical imbalances in my brain, and how being a teenager is practically a form of mental illness. She didn't say anything (I mean, what is there to say?), but just collapsed in a heap of human tiredness next to me.

Now we're scrunched into VERY uncomfortable seats in the middle of this HUGE plane. I asked my mother why we couldn't get window seats, and she started talking about airlines and hubs and cruise packages, so I told her to never mind. To make matters worse, my head is killing me. I think it's doing the same thing as this water bottle I have here. When the plane took off, it started bloating out like it would explode (the water bottle, not the plane) (luckily). It was like that until I opened the top to drink some, and then it went back to its normal size. I wonder if it would help my head if I could open the top of it like that. (Clearly, I am experiencing oxygen depletion or something, so don't mind me.)

I started watching the movie to distract myself, but then I realized that it's one of those flicks about a beautiful model-like woman falling in love with a gray, wrinkled guy. I'm trying not to look at it, because I know she's bound to kiss him at any moment—argh! (Or, as Georgia would say: erlack!) Even though I'm listening to music now on my headphones, I guess Mom thinks I'm still listening to the movie, because every once in a while she looks over at me and giggles— figuring, I guess, that we are sharing some girlish thoughts about the movie. (Yeah . . . uh-HUH.)

OMG! The person in front of me just threw up! This is worse than the movie! Get me OUT of here! Wait a minute! I'm on an AIRPLANE! I can't go ANYWHERE! OK, I'll just get OUT OF THIS SEAT and walk up and down the aisle for the next six hours or however long it'll be before we get to Rome. OMG again! The food and drink carts are back! I'm STUCK! HELP! THEY'RE GOING TO EEEAATTTT MEEEEEE!!

Wishing you were here,

Brady

Dear Delia,

I've never been so tired in my whole, entire life. Not even the time you made me stay up all night before that all-day band performance. (NO, I haven't gotten over that yet.) I feel like an old sock that's been worn by a hundred people, then dragged along the street for a few years, then stomped on by elephants, then used to clean toilets. In the boys' locker room.

That was the worst flight EVER. You should have seen my water bottle squeezing in when we were landing in Rome. My head was squeezing in like that, too. You know those little toys with the eyeballs made of goo that pop out when you squish the head? Well, my head did that. My eyeballs were on the floor. Really. REALLY. (Okay, FINE, don't believe me.)

When we got off the plane, we were greeted by a brigade of smiling Italian teenage boys in berets and uniforms. I immediately thought, "Delia would LOVE it here!" A couple of them smiled at me, even, and winked, and I started thinking that maybe it wasn't going to be so hard to find Euro-hotties, after all. I was so completely out of it from sleep deprivation and the head-squeezing thing that I careened right over to where they were standing and started to actually introduce myself (although I'm not entirely sure I remembered my own name at that point). THEN I noticed the guns. Each of those cute Italian guys was carrying a MAJOR automatic rifle. You KNOW how I HATE guns.

(Well, you wouldn't want me compromising my beliefs just to meet a Euro-hottie, now, would you?) (Of course you would.)

"It's because of terrorism, dear," my mother whispered pseudo-calmly as she guided me (with a death-grip on my arm) past the guns-and-berets guys.

Then we got on yet ANOTHER form of transportation. I bet you can't guess how many different ways I've traveled since I left DC. Hey, I know! I'll give you a quiz:

To get from Washington, DC, to a cruise ship near Rome, you must:

a) ride in a car

b) walk

c) run

d) use one of those people-mover-floors that are like escalators, only flat

e) use an escalator (would the verb be "escalate"?)

f) use an elevator (elevate?)

g) fly in an airplane

h) take a bus

i) all of the above

Well, here's the answer: (i) all of the above. SERIOUSLY.

We're on a bus now, heading for a seaside town near Rome. It's called Civitavecchia (pronounced CHEE-vit-a-vekkia), according to my mother, who asked me to practice saying it. I refused, though, on account that there is no reason for me to know how to say the name of this town. We're going there to get on the boat, and then the boat LEAVES there. It seems to me that I'll only need to say the town's name if I happen to fall out the window of this bus and then have to tell someone where to take me when they pick me up hitch-hiking. The window next to my seat is about six inches square, so I don't think I'll be falling out of it today.

So, HERE I AM in ITALY! I guess it's time to describe some thrilling adventures! Well, I'm looking out the window, and I can see a, uh, road. There are cars and buses. And it's really, really hot here. I don't think there's air-conditioning on this bus. Which is making me pretty sleepy. Really sleepy. Really, REALLY sleepy. Oh, look! It's the ocean! I've never seen that EXCELLENT shade of blue . . .

Sunday
(*I know this because the mat outside
the elevator in the ship says so*)

Dear Delia,

Oh, my. I must have fallen asleep writing that last letter. I woke up and my pen was smashed against my cheek. I haven't been able to get rid of the purple mark it left there, so this morning I turned it into a little heart. But I thought that looked silly, and, anyway, I remembered that purple hearts are things that soldiers are given when they get injured in war, and it didn't seem right to have one on my face. So I made it into a circle, which looked REAL silly, because why would a person have a purple CIRCLE on her face? So I got my blue pen and made petals around the circle, and now I have a flower on my cheek. It looks really, well, RIDICULOUS. I tried to scrub it off, but it's no use, and now my cheek is red. With a purple and blue flower on it. My sunglasses cover it just a little, but not nearly enough. I sure hope I don't run into, uh, ANYONE.

It is PARADISE here, Delia, let me tell you. The sun is shining, and here I am, next to a sparkling pool, looking at Mount Vesuvius and listening to a Caribbean band. (And wondering if this band realizes they are on the wrong sea.) I slept twelve hours last night and then ran some laps on the top deck of the boat, gazing out at the INCREDIBLE, hypnotic BLUE of the Mediterranean. It doesn't look at all like the Atlantic Ocean. It's SO much darker. Somewhere between Hope-diamond blue and midnight blue. How nice it is to be surrounded by all this blueness. Mediterranean blue is my NEW favorite shade of BLUE.

I am TOTALLY rejuvenated now, and except for the obnoxious flower on my cheek, and the stupid writing all over my hand, life is GREAT. I'm actually wearing the bikini today, Delia, BELIEVE it or not. (SEE? I'm making progress with the LIST.) I put it on and looked in the mirror of our stateroom (that's cruise-speak for bedroom), and I started to think that maybe I didn't look too awfully bad in it, and I was STEPPING OUT of the cute, little door (which makes it seem like we're living in a hobbit hole), when my mother said, "You know, Brady, you really HAVE developed quite a bit lately." At which point, I grabbed a big T-shirt from my bag and put it over the bikini.

SORRY. I'm just not ready. There's NOTHING wrong with swimming in a T-shirt, anyway. So WHAT if it gets caught up around your neck and keeps your arms from going over your head when you're trying to do the freestyle? Who CARES if it bloats up and makes you look like a blowfish when you're doing the backstroke? What of it?

Through the fog of jet lag, I am starting to remember some things about yesterday's arrival at port. It wasn't "thrilling," but I'm going to tell you about it anyway. In Civitavecchia, we went to this building at the docks, where bunches of people were sitting around on benches with their suitcases, all looking extremely tired. Every once in a while, someone in a uniform called out a number or a letter or something, and people slowly got up and grabbed their suitcases, woke up their other family members, and schlepped (as my grandmother says), slow motion, across the hot room and into a line.

I watched this for a while, and in my quasi-sleep-state I was convinced I was on Ellis Island. It made perfect sense, too—at least in the la-la land I was in. It was not air and land travel which had worn me out, but TIME travel. I was a composite of my ancestors who had journeyed from Russia and Germany and Ireland, sick of Cossacks and Nazis and bad potatoes. I was ONE with their struggles. That IS, until I fell asleep again on my backpack.

I woke up thinking about those ancestors this morning. I felt, at first, kind of guilty, because they were poor immigrants, and they couldn't afford to take vacations, I'm sure. Of course, they probably would have had no interest at all in going back across the Atlantic to get on a BOAT, of all things. And the more I thought about it, the more I realized that my great-great-grandparents (or whoever) would be really happy if they knew I was able to take such a COOL trip. It would mean that their idea to come to America had been a good one. Right? Didn't they want their descendants to have better lives? Wasn't that the point?

Okay. I'm done with that now. I feel better.

The ship sailed during the night and arrived early this morning in the port of Naples, Italy. My mother keeps saying we should go see the city, but I keep saying we should stay at the pool for a while longer. The water is actually very cold in the pool, and—here's a shocker—it's salty. This weirded me out at first, but then some waiter-type person who was delivering drinks with little umbrellas (the drinks had the little umbrellas, not the waiter-type person) told us that the pool is emptied every night and then filled up with water right out of the sea. Is that cool, or what? (Cold, actually. As I've already said.)

"What about Pompeii?" my mother has just suggested.

Pompeii! Now, THAT has potential. Lost world and all.

Ciao, baby!

Brady

Dear Delia,

Pompeii is very cool, a little weird, and decidedly creepy.

Except for all the roofs being gone from every building, the town looks just as it did in 79 AD right before it was covered in spewing ash. (Spewing Ash . . . that would be a good name for a band, don't you think?) It was there one day—a regular Italian town with, like, 20,000 people living in it—and then it WASN'T there. It was HISTORY. (Hehe.)

We took this bus there with an Italian guide who had one of those hairdos that's parted real far over on the side and then lopped over the top of the head, very convincingly (NON) covering up a humongoid bald spot. His name was Sergio.

He gave us stickers to wear—big, round, green things with white numbers on them. I was number 11, and—choosing not to put this big round thing on my top, for fear of drawing unneeded attention to my, uh, TOP—I placed it on the right butt of my shorts. Which, for some reason, caused a reaction from my mother.

"Brady," she said, "do you think that's appropriate?"

"What's wrong with wearing a sticker on the right butt of my shorts?" I asked her.

"It's just, somehow, inappropriate," she said.

(I know what I'm getting her for her birthday. A thesaurus, so she can find some synonyms for "inappropriate." This is becoming tiresome.)

Even though I did NOT get what the problem was, I decided to be an accommodating daughter. I peeled the sticker off the right butt of my shorts and put it in a different place. The left butt of my shorts.

Her reaction to this was a LOOK and a gesture with her hand. But since I don't have ESP, and I'm not fluent in sign language (her hand-wave looked something like the one I've seen for the word "elephant" . . . or maybe it's "cabbage"), I had no choice but to ignore her.

I did end up moving the sticker again, but it was not because of my mother. It was because of Sergio.

You see, he said something in Italian to us as we were taking our seats on the bus, IN FRONT (mio madre's idea— PLEASE!), which my mother scrambled to translate from the Italian phrase book. But before she found anything, he WINKED at her and repeated what he said, in English, with a major Italian accent (probably fake, just to impress tourists), which was, "Beautiful ladies, welcome!"

Then he touched his cheek, looked at me, and said something else in Italian, laughing in an Italian sort of way. I stared at him like he was from Mars (which I think he may be), while my mother flipped through the book again. Of course, he translated himself before she could find any of the words. (WHY, exactly, was he speaking in two languages?) Touching his cheek again he said to me, "Flower child?" and laughed some more. I grabbed the phrase book from Mom and began to search for the Italian word for "moron" (which, by the way, is NOT in there—what a useless book), but by then he had taken up the microphone and was speaking to the busload of people in some combination of Italian and English (and Martian).

"Your little flower's cute," my mother whispered to me.

CUTE. Yes, I strive for CUTE. And I especially want people of the boomer generation to think I am CUTE. So I peeled the number sticker off my shorts and put it over the flower on my cheek.

I know that made no sense. But it was somehow satisfying.

When we got to Pompeii, Sergio displayed more mad tendencies by producing from under his seat a red umbrella. There was not a cloud in the sky, but he carried this umbrella around Pompeii. I did find it useful, though, since I made the decision early on that I was going to stay as far from him as possible, and the red umbrella served as sort of a flag to show me where he was, so I could hang back a bit and not get lost. In the lost city. (Hehe.)

We first went to Pompeii's Forum, which is a Roman-type gathering place—sort of like the grass fields on the Mall at the Washington Monument. We had a perfect view of the mountain, and Sergio (in too lively a tone, I think) told us what it was like for the people of Pompeii the day they got buried by the volcano. He described (with flourishes) how the Pompeians stood right where we were standing, probably talking about ordinary things and enjoying the view, when the ground started to shake. Then, before they could get home to their families or find their best friends, the top of Vesuvius blew off in an enormous explosion of lava, and even though the mountain was a few miles away, darkness (he said brightly) fell over Pompeii within MINUTES, and 20 feet of ash covered the city within hours. And then it was all quiet. Very quiet. Very, VERY quiet. And it stayed like that, forgotten in time, until the 1700s, when someone was out digging a hole and found the place.

I saw some of the original Pompeii people while I was there. And I don't mean ghosts, either. I saw THE PEOPLE. Well, OKAY, they were models. You see, the archaeologists who dug out Pompeii found lots of bodies, but there wasn't much left of them, except these perfect outlines of their shapes in hardened ash. So they filled the outlines up with plaster and made casts of the people. There are a couple of buildings that have these people-casts in them, frozen in time, running, hugging other people. Molto eerie.

We also saw the Coliseum—where Pompeians went to watch gladiator fights and other sports events—and we saw the Public Baths. There didn't seem to be any bathrooms in the houses of Pompeii, so these were places where the people went to bathe together in large tubs. (Thankfully, there were none of those plaster-casts in that building.) I can't really remember all the other places we went to, because Pompeii is HUGE, and since there are basically no trees and no ceilings, the Italian sun (which seems to be a little hotter than ours) was frying my brain. I do remember some frescoes we saw, so I will tell you about those. First, I'm guessing I need to tell you what frescoes ARE.

Frescoes, Delia, are murals that Italians have been painting forever and ever. They have some way of getting the paint to bleed into the wall, which sounds weird but seems to work pretty well, seeing how the frescoes of Pompeii were put there before 79 AD, then had a volcano erupt all over them, then were buried in ash for about 1,700 years, then were dug out and looked at by tourists for another 200 years or so, and the pictures are STILL there.

My fave fresco was at the House of Venus, and it was of—can you guess?—VENUS, lounging about in a large seashell, attended by cupids and little flittering birdies. The painting is on a wall in what used to be a garden, and the background is a faded but very cool BLUE, with Venus in the center, all spiffed-up in a necklace and some sort of tiara. (You do know I'm talking about the GODDESS Venus, not the planet, right?)

The last frescoes I saw were at a house called the Villa of Mysteries. It is named this because the frescoes there tell a story that is—can you guess this, too?—a MYSTERY! These are BIG murals with a BRIGHT red background and larger-than-life-size people in a series of panels that go all around the room, telling some kind of tale. Sort of like a comic strip. Only—believe me—you'd never see THESE in your Sunday paper.

Sergio may have been making this up (one can hope), but he said the murals represent an "ancient spiritual document" having to do with Dionysus, a god that was supposedly born from Zeus's thigh. (Yes, I said THIGH.) The pictures, he told us (a little too enthusiastically), are all about rituals done in honor of this god—rituals like torture, animal sacrifices, and drinking blood.

I'm sure you are molto disappointed, Delia, but I can't tell you anything else about the story, because when Sergio got to that last part, the panini I had eaten for lunch started rumbling in my stomach, and fearing that it would be the next thing spewing all over Pompeii, I headed for the door.

(Uh, there aren't really doors in Pompeii, but you know what I mean.) Before I made it outside, though, I bumped into my mother. This was a good thing, because I had something I needed to ask her.

"Madre," I said, pointing (but not looking) at the paintings of naked, terror-stricken Pompeians being whipped and drugged by satyrs (those half-man, half-goat things) or devils or something. "Do you think that's appropriate?"

She was non-responsive. (Catatonic, I think.)

Before we left Pompeii, we went to the gift shop so I could find a postcard of the Venus fresco to send you, but the first card I saw was of the Dionysus murals, so I had to run from the shop, screaming. (Okay, not really, but in my mind I did.)

Guess what? I have just found some interesting Italian sentences in my mother's little book, in a chapter entitled, COMMON PHRASES NEEDED BY TRAVELERS. Here's a good one: "Dov'e la passerella?" It means "where is the gangplank?" And how about this one: "C'e tropp'acqua nella barca." That means "there's too much water in the boat."

Do you find it troubling that these are considered "common phrases?" I do. Especially since I just heard the ship's horn, which means we're heading out into open water.

Tomorrow we'll be at sea all day, and then we get to Barcelona the next day. (That's in Spain, Delia.) But right now, I'm STARVED, so we are going to the dining room. Then there's a party in the teen lounge, according to this little invitation I found on my bed when we got back to the stateroom today. It was under the claw of a lizard, which our porter (in land-speak: butler) had somehow made from a bath towel. I don't know if I'm going to the party or not. Mom says there are teen parties every night, so I'll have other chances.

I'm kind of tired, anyway.

It's MY vacation, after all.

I don't have to do anything I don't want to do.

I might want to READ or something, you know.

Okay. I'm SCARED to go. I've SAID it. So leave me alone.

Brady

p.s. I SAID, LEAVE ME ALONE!

Dear Delia,

I've just changed clothes to get ready for the party. Aren't you proud of me? The black tank top I wore to dinner just wasn't cutting it. It's been tight anyway, lately, and after eating lasagna, salad, bread, cheesecake, and two iced teas—they stuff you like pigs here—I thought the seams would pop. Which can be VERY dangerous when you're at a party, you have to admit. So, after rooting through my suitcase and trying on every top I brought with me, I finally picked a shirt that is sure to boost my confidence tonight: my favorite baseball jersey! Number 12!

I hit four homeruns in this shirt, seven doubles, and one triple, so I think it should help me through a simple, little party. I've GOT my GAME on, Delia! I am GONE!

Hm. I'm still here. Maybe while I'm waiting for the cheerleaders and marching band to arrive, I could write a bit more to you about, uh, DINNER—

Yes, that! Tonight was the first time we had dinner in the big dining room, where we're supposed to eat every night. We watched Mount Vesuvius fade into the distance through these huge windows (or else they're pretty MAJOR flat-screen TVs), while a string quartet played in the background. Our waiter is this cute, old Greek guy with a black shawl, named Cristo. (The waiter is named Cristo, not the shawl.) He's got to be at least eighty, or maybe a hundred, and you can barely hear him when he speaks, so we all had to lean over each other to find out what the two dinner choices were. The only thing I could understand was "lasagna," so I ordered that. Good thing—it turned out the other was some vegetarian pilaf, or something, because this one woman at our table ended up with that on her plate. It looked WAY too healthy for a vacation food.

The pilaf woman is named Linn, and she's Vietnamese and was at the table with her husband and son—also Vietnamese—

who didn't say much. I think they only speak their native language, which is (I'm sure you guessed this) French. They live in Paris. My mother asked Linn where they live in Paris, and she answered, "Chinatown, of course," with more than a hint of "DUH."

I've been thinking about this. She obviously thought my mother's question was silly. I thought it was silly, too, but that's because I knew she asked it just to have something to say, and not because the answer would mean anything to her. A response like, "I live on Lafayette Boulevard," would have produced a politely enthusiastic nod from my mother and an immediate insertion of a large forkful of lasagna into her mouth, to cover up the fact that she knows absolutely nothing about the neighborhoods of Paris. But Linn didn't know that. She just seemed to think that my mother should have assumed her family lives in Chinatown. Uh, WHY? Aren't Vietnam and China two completely different countries? I mean, do all Asian people live in ONE place in Paris?

Delia, you're probably thinking, "Why is Brady asking ME these questions?" Or you COULD be thinking, "Why doesn't Brady stop procrastinating and GET TO THE PARTY???" (To either question, my answer is the same: I don't know.)

Linn's son is fifteen, and she told us his full name, which is something like Linn Chi Lahn. And, yes, it seemed strange that a boy would have the same first name as his mother, but then Linn explained that Vietnamese names are sort of backwards, and the first name is actually at the end, so he is called Lahn. My mother, then, wanted to know why she was called Linn (though if I were her, I would have been afraid of somehow appearing stupid again, but we're talking my mother here), and Linn explained that her name was reversed when her family first immigrated to France, so she just got used to being called Linn.

I remembered that something like that happened with my grandmother's family. I don't think they even had a last name, because they came from a shtetl a long time ago, where last names weren't even used, and they ended up being called "Goldsmith" because, I guess, they WERE goldsmiths. So, anyway, I thought the Vietnamese name thing was kind of cool, since— as your message on my hand continues to remind me—I like to learn things. I was thinking of one of your other messages on my hand, though, when I first saw Lahn at the table tonight and asked myself, "Is this a code-red Euro-hottie sitting RIGHT here at my dinner table?"

I have decided that, no, he is not code-red material. Orange, maybe, but that's not enough for you, I guess. He is tall and nice-looking, but there's a pretty significant language barrier, and I have to draw the line there. I mean, if I can't talk to someone, at least a little bit, they CAN'T be code-red, and that's THAT. YOU might be able to rate someone strictly on the basis of appearance, but that's because you are superficial and I am not.

This is so much fun—being able to say things like that, without you punching me in the arm.

Hm. But what if I am already home and sitting next to you as you're reading this? I suppose, in that case, I am running out of the room.

ANYWAY. I personally need to know there are attractive thoughts inside an attractive head. Or, in the absence of that, I'd want him to perform some sort of athletic feat. (And, Delia, I'm not talking what's inside his shoes. Definitely not that.) I did, for a moment, think that I might be able to communicate with Lahn, though, when his mother said, "Lahn speaks English." But then Lahn gave his mother the same look I give my mother when she tells people I speak German just because I've taken it for one year at school. Some things are the same all over the planet, I suppose. Like the look you are required to give your parents when they act like they have recently escaped from the psych ward.

Guess what I found out? (I know you don't care, but tough.) We are supposed to eat at the same table every night, with the same people. It's like they're our boat-family, or something. It's a pretty adult-heavy family, though—Lahn and I are the only kids. There is this couple from Canada, who have EXCELLENT Canadian accents, and these two grandparent-type women from California, who have California accents, which is to say they have no accents. Don't you think it's weird that certain parts of our country have MAJOR accents—like Alabama and Massachusetts and North Dakota— and other places have NO accents?

Okay, okay. I'm sure, by now, you are screaming at the top of your lungs, "STOP <u>THINKING</u>, AND GO TO THE STINK-ING <u>PARTY</u>!!!" Yes, you're right. My mother went to a show with her Canadian siblings, so it's pretty lonely here, just me and the pile of clothes that spilled out of my suitcase. Maybe I should put them away before I go.

Nah. It makes me feel like I'm in my room at home, which is soothing. I could, though, put some more concealer over my cheek-flower. Between that and all the words on my hand, I feel like one of those tattoo-obsessed people. Which doesn't help with my confidence level, LET ME TELL YOU.

Oh, all right, all right. I'm GOING, I'm GOING.

Brady (a.k.a. Painted Lady)

Sunday, still
(Will it never end?)

Dear Delia,

I'm pathetic. You should start proceedings to divorce me as your best friend, because there is no hope for me. Ever. You should have seen me at the teen party tonight. It was total, public humiliation. I would jump overboard, but then there'd be the bigger public humiliation of a rescue. Running away once we land in Barcelona may be my only option. I can't write this letter now, because I have to pack.

Oh, OKAY. I'll tell you about it. (THEN I'll pack.)

THE PARTY

Everything started out FINE. I took the elevator to deck nine, where the teen lounge is, and the party was already going on. I was greeted by Pink's voice over the speakers (GET THIS PARTY STARTED!!) and a very happy-looking guy in a sailor hat. (The little white type of sailor hat, like the one I bought for my five-year-old cousin when I was on the Cape May ferry last summer.) I can't remember the guy's name, so I'll call him Gilligan.

"Hello!" Gilligan said, all excitedly. "I'm the youth activity director!"

"Hi," I said, noticing immediately that there were several foosball tables at one end of the room. There were only a few gamers at each one—all boys, perhaps even some Euro-hotties, I figured—so I began to think that maybe this wouldn't be so hard, after all. I'm pretty good at foosball, and I'm way more comfortable in a competitive sort of atmosphere. My confidence was building, Delia.

"Drinks and snacks over there," Gilligan said cheerfully, pointing in the direction of a long bar, where there were sodas all lined up and glass bowls filled with—this is awesome—Mediterranean blue M&Ms. He started to say something else, but was interrupted when one of the gamers suddenly yelled, "TOURNAMENT!" which resulted in just about everyone in the room heading over to watch the foosball players. It was like some huge magnets inside the tables had been activated.

So, figuring I'd wait till the crowd died down over there, I headed to the bar. First I downed a big handful of the blue M&Ms (for courage) and then looked over the sodas. Each had a maraschino cherry floating on top and a plastic animal hanging over the rim of the glass. I took one with a cute, little monkey.

(In retrospect, I'm thinking that was a poor choice, given what happened next. Clearly, monkeys are bad karma for me— maybe a giraffe would have been better.)

By the bar was a wall that showed music videos, and a few girls were dancing in front of it. Near them were a few puffy chairs, and one of them was occupied by a boy with dark, wavy hair and dark eyes. Italian, I figured. Or Greek. Or Israeli. Or some similarly attractive alien species. I sized him up, Delia, as almost certainly code-red. And all I needed to do, I told myself, was walk up and meet him. THEN, I told myself, task #4 on Delia's (annoying) to-do list would be OVER. There was one little problem, though: TOTAL PANIC.

Feeling like I would throw up any second, I asked myself (not out loud, thankfully), "What would Delia do?" Naturally, the answer terrified me, so I switched to the question: "What would Georgia do?" To that, I thought-answered, "Well, she would be British, of course, and I know how to do THAT." And then I thought-added, "But what if he doesn't speak English? Or British, for that matter?" At which point, I thought-yelled, "DO IT, BRADY!"

So, armed with this (totally misplaced) sense of confidence, I strolled over to the puffy orange chair and, acting like a cool person (which I'm obviously NOT), picked the cherry out of my glass, popped it into my mouth, and said, "Bazzin' pahty!" (Which I know is stupid, but it made perfect sense in the completely idiotic fantasy world I had entered by then.)

He turned, smiling, and said, in a definitely too-loud kind of way, and in a cowboy accent straight out of the Wild West, "Hey! Yer a New Yorker!"

At which moment I inhaled the maraschino cherry and began to CHOKE. I couldn't get a sound out at first, and I guess this guy is trained in life-saving or something, because he sprang right up out of his seat and got behind me and squeezed my stomach so hard that the cherry FLEW out of my mouth. At that point I managed to squeak out, "I'm okay!" so he let me go. By then the girls on the dance floor had stopped dancing and were looking at us, as was the rest of the room. (And the rest of the world, I think.)

"Ma name's AJ," he said, smiling (a little too) big. "Ahm from Texas. I lak that flar on yer face."

Still feeling somewhat gaggy, I coughed out, "Thanks!" and "Got to go!" and "Bye!" until I backed myself to the lounge door, at which point I bolted for the elevator, which didn't come fast enough, so I ran down a thousand flights of stairs (at least) and all the way back to our stateroom, where, panting, I jumped into bed.

I'm so pitiful that I'm clearly a hazard to myself.

And I'm NEVER going to be British again. Speaking that way is EXHAUSTING, anyway. I don't know how the Brits do it all day.

And I also don't GET how the Queen's husband can be a prince. Shouldn't he be the KING? Georgia may be the only thing that makes sense over there, and she's not even REAL.

My mother just got back from the show. She's telling me to get my clothes off the floor. I'm telling her that I'm just trying to make it more like home, so she'll be cozy and not get homesick. She doesn't seem to appreciate that, though, because she keeps telling me to get out of bed and pick up my clothes. See if I do anything nice for her again.

Dov'e la passerella?

Brady

Dear Delia,

It is our day at sea. I haven't seen land since we passed Sicily last night. We cruise very fast—it's like we're not even touching the water. No waves chop up the surface, and the only white I can see on the dark blue sea is this foamy trail of a V that the boat leaves behind. It makes me think of UVA basketball camp. (Because all their athletic stuff has a big "V" on it. You know, for Virginia?)

Mom is very busy this morning reading up on Barcelona and planning some "exciting sightseeing activities" (!) for our day tomorrow. Perhaps it was the psycho Pompeian tour guide, but she has made the suggestion that we explore the rest of the cities on our own. I told her I thought that was a fine idea, but she insisted on having a conversation about it anyway. It went like this:

MOM: We have to be back at the boat by a certain time each day, and if we miss it, it sails without us. Should we worry about that?

ME: Uh, no.

MOM: It might be dangerous, too, don't you think? Two women, alone in strange cities?

ME: How does that work, exactly? Being alone when you're two women?

She tried to hand me a book on Barcelona today, but I refused to read it on the grounds that it is—quite obviously—totally bad luck to study anything when you're on vacation. (See? I'm not THAT much of a geek.) At this moment she is trying to find a subway map, or something, in the ship's Internet Café. Which reminds me—I must send an e-mail to my little sister, because I promised I would tell her what it's like in a different country, since she's never been, well, anywhere.

(I'm not entirely sure she's ever been away from her computer, actually.) The story of my day in Pompeii would be rated PG-13, though, so she's too young for that. And the story of the party last night would be rated R (for ridiculous), so I'm NOT writing to her—or ANYONE—about that. (Well, except you, obviously). I guess I'll have to wait until I have a normal experience, which might take a while, the way things are going.

Actually, there has been a small improvement in my life this morning. I have almost completely rid my face of the flower. I put a layer of sunscreen on it, let it set for a half hour, then massaged it in for a minute or two, then wiped it off with a tissue. Then, feeling a lot like a person in an infomercial, I scrubbed in a circular motion twenty times with glycerin soap. I think I look pretty good today, and if it weren't for the fact that I have to stay hidden and in disguise, I would be ready to go out in public again.

I have found a deck with no (cool) people on it—deck six— and I am hunkered down in a lounge chair. I have a visor and dark sunglasses on and a shirt I had not yet worn on the boat (which was not hard, since it's only the third day of our cruise). Earlier, I tried running on this deck, but some very tanned, blond-haired, oldish women told me it was a "power-walking only" deck. (Which probably has something to do with there being no cool people anywhere near it.)

Oh, no! Some girls are approaching. They look vaguely familiar. Must be from the party last night.

Bye! Gotta pretend I'm dead!

Brady

Monday night

Dear Delia,

I only have a moment, but thought I'd tell you about the major (and very strange) improvement in my situation aboard the boat. It seems I have somehow achieved celebrity status. Those girls I saw this morning? Well, they were actually LOOKING for me. You see, after the maraschino cherry incident, AJ—according to the girls—was very upset that I'd left. Seems he, uh, FANCIES me. He was asking all the other people in the lounge if they knew my name, and of course, no one did, since I don't (didn't) know a single soul on the boat. So, he said he was going to find me, and he asked for help.

(I feel like Cinderella. Only instead of leaving a shoe at the party, the only thing I left was a masticated cherry. Now, THERE'S an image: Prince AJ knocking on stateroom doors, maraschino cherry in hand, trying to find the girl with the dainty throat that fits the cherry. Okay. I know that's weird.)

The girls who informed me of this situation were speaking perfect English and wearing shirts with the words "USA!" and "America Rocks" on the fronts, so I assumed they were fellow Americans. How foolish I am! They are—of course!—Lebanese. (The foreign language programs in Lebanon are obviously far superior to ours in America, judging by the degree of fluency they have in English, which about matches the degree of non-fluency I have in German.) They told me this whole story of what transpired at the party after my getaway. At the end of it, they said, simultaneously, "You are SO lucky! Don't you think AJ's HOT?"

"Uh, NO?" I said. Then noticing their expressions of aghast-ness (is that a word?), I added, "You see, I'm from Washington, DC, and we, uh, don't really, uh, GET the Texans—yeah, THAT."

"Really?" the girl who had introduced herself as Tatyana asked, smiling.

"So, you don't LIKE him?" Noori (the other girl) (duh) asked.

"Well, I like him in a he's-pretty-good-at-the-Heimlich-maneuver sort of way," I said, "But, no, I don't LIKE him like him."

"So, can my best friend, Noori, ask him out?" Tatyana asked.

"Okaay," I said, wondering when I'd been appointed Love Czar of the cruise.

"Oh, THANKS!" Noori said. And she actually HUGGED me.

(Hormones rage in Lebanon, too, I guess.)

"So, I'm wondering," I said, "how did you get both of your families to go on the same vacation?"

"We're with my parents," Tatyana said. "Next month we're doing the eastern Mediterranean with Noori's parents."

"We don't have any brothers or sisters, so we've been going on vacations together for forever," Noori added.

"You are really lucky," I said. "If my best friend were here, I know I'd have SO much more fun."

(Which is true, Delia.)

(Even though you are SUCH a pain.)

"Do stuff with us!" Noori said.

"Yeah," Tatyana said. "Meet us at the party tonight, at the Roman Ruins Pool."

"Okay," I said. "That's REALLY nice."

"So," Tatyana said, after a pause, "is it, um, a GOOD thing to be a geeky jock in DC?"

I realized then that the palm of my hand was openly displayed on the arm of my lounge chair, so, quickly flipping it over, I said, laughing, "Oh, that was written by a person I was visiting in a mental institution."

(Well, THAT'S what you get for using a Sharpie and going over the letters so many times. I think I may have this on my hand for LIFE.)

Then my NEW FRIENDS—who don't WRITE on me, thank-you-very-much—and I hung out and did some scheming about how to get AJ to shift his amore (that's LOVE) from me to Noori.

Speaking of WHICH . . . I've gotta go! I'm supposed to meet them early, so I can tell them about Texas.

Which might be difficult, since I've never BEEN there.

Life is a very bizarre thing, isn't it?

Bye, now!

Brady

p.s. I am wearing the bikini!

p.p.s. But I put a shirt over it again.

p.p.p.s. SORRY! I'm JUST NOT READY!

p.p.p.p.s. Anyway, with this Texas guy out looking for me, I don't think I should wear something that might further attract his attention.

p.p.p.p.p.s. AND YOU CAN'T DO ANYTHING ABOUT IT BECAUSE YOU'RE THOUSANDS OF MILES AWAY!

p.p.p.p.p.p.s. I know, I KNOW. I'm truly sad. (Sigh.)

Tuesday (or so the mat says)

Dear Delia,

I woke up to the sight of land out of the porthole (in Earth-speak: window). We are arriving in Barcelona. Mi madre (which looks a lot like Italian, I know, but it is pronounced "mee MAH-dray," and it is Spanish, since we are in . . . YES! SPAIN!) has informed me that we have to eat a "quick-quick" breakfast, so we can get ashore. We have, she says, exactly six hours to cover "a whole list of must-sees." Then she read them off to me, but I can't tell you what they were, because I was thinking about something else at the time. Like how much I like to sleep when I'm tired. Then she ran off and said we would be leaving "the moment" she gets back. I'm sure I have time, though, to squeeze in a teeny-weeny report on . . .

THE POSEIDON MIXER

Which is what the party was called last night—at least according to the banner over the entrance to the Roman Ruins Pool. Standing under it, greeting us, was Gilligan, the social director dude.

He pointed to the banner and told us—with oodles of enthusiasm—that he'd made it himself on the computer. We complimented him—what a cool font he'd chosen, what excellent colors, what realistic waves, and what an awesome Poseidon! You know, the usual humoring-of-adults drill.

"You're the first ones to greet Poseidon, the god who reigns over the mixer, triton in hand!" he said, pointing then to the middle of the pool, where a large statue of a sea god loomed over the water.

"But isn't that three-pronged thing called a trident?" Tatyana asked him.

"No, no, it's a triton," Gilligan said in an aren't-you-silly-kids sort of way.

"I thought Triton was the name of his kid," I said. "The half-fish one."

"Yes!" Noori said. "Triton was the king in <u>The Little Mermaid</u>!"

Gilligan was momentarily flustered, then smiled and proclaimed, "And Poseidon is the king of the mixer!"

We smiled back and nodded slowly. (In a universal-sign-for-kookoo sort of way.)

He pulled some wristbands from a bag he was carrying and started to tell us about a "big surprise" he had planned for the evening, when Tatyana said, "Are you really sure that's even a statue of Poseidon?"

"Yes! Poseidon's the god of the sea!" he answered. "You should each take a different color wristband, and be listening for a—"

"Poseidon's from Greek mythology, though," Noori said, interrupting him. "Isn't this the Roman Ruins Pool?"

"I think that's really Neptune," I threw in.

"The Roman sea god," Tatyana added.

(You know, the informing-adults-of-things-they-should-already-know drill.)

Some new people arrived just about then, and Gilligan—with an extremely relieved look on his face—began greeting them.

The wristbands he gave us are like those Livestrong things, only they were in a bunch of different colors, and they said "Poseidon's Mixer" on them. I took a blue one (of course), Noori got orange, and Tatyana pink.

We staked out some lounge chairs and listened to the music the DJ was playing, which was mostly rap. Lahn showed up, and I waved him over to a chair by ours. (Lahn is the one from our dinner table, in case you're having a hard time keeping up with my rapidly increasing social circle). Then AJ appeared, of course, so we put PHASE ONE of our plan into action. It went like this:

1. AJ makes a beeline to me.
2. I thank him for being such a cool guy and saving my life.
3. He asks me if I want to dance.
4. I say, "No, thank you."
5. He asks me if I want to swim.
6. I say, "No, thank you."

7. Noori announces she is going swimming, takes off her batik wrap to display a red, white, and blue string bikini, and dives into the pool. (Which was really smooth, Delia. You would like this girl.)

8. PHASE ONE ends—and fails—when AJ does not follow her, but remains lodged next to my lounge chair.

9. There is no PHASE TWO.

So we just hung out in our lounge chairs—Lahn, Tatyana, Noori (who gave up on the swim pretty quickly), and me, with AJ standing RIGHT next to my chair, like a bodyguard. It was <u>muy</u> (that's Spanish for "very") uncomfortable.

Finally, Noori said, "Anyone thirsty?" and everyone said YES at the exact same time. So she headed off to the poolside bar for drinks.

Seeing a potential opportunity in this, I said, to no one in particular, "That's a lot of drinks to carry."

And, as I expected (because he's such a helpful guy—it's really too bad I find him kind of repulsive), AJ said, "Ahl help," and he trotted off after Noori.

"So, do you have a boyfriend in DC?" Tatyana asked, as we watched AJ pulsing off into the now strobe-lit distance.

"No," I told her. Then thinking about the gift you gave me for my birthday, I added, "But I grew one once."

She gave me an odd look—as you might imagine—then seemed to catch on to what I was saying. "Oh, the 'Grow-a-Boyfriend' thing, right? I had one once. They're fun!"

"TRULY," I said. And then I told her about how you and I stuck mine in water but didn't realize the head wasn't submerged, and the next day we pulled him out, and he'd grown, like, eight times his original size and was really, really buff, except his head was the size of a pea. And I told her how, after we discovered THAT, we started experimenting with him—only his legs in the water, then only his feet, then one arm.

As you would guess, Tatyana and I were cracking up at these mental images of the various Grow-a-Boyfriend morphs, and when I got to the description of the HUGE-head version, and how YOU thought he looked like Marvin the Martian, but I thought he looked like Linus, she TOTALLY lost it and rolled right off her chair and into Lahn (who had been pretty much ignoring us during the whole episode).

"Oops, sorry!" she said, climbing back up on the chair.

We both looked over and smiled at him, and he smiled back, but quickly looked away. We couldn't help but notice that he'd turned COMPLETELY red.

"Do you think he was offended by the Grow-a-Boyfriend thing?" Tatyana whispered to me.

"He doesn't speak English," I said. "I'm sure he just thinks we're weird."

"Yeah," Tatyana said, letting out a big sigh. After a couple of seconds she added, "So, what's California like?"

(Which was kind of RANDOM, wouldn't you say?)

"Well," I said, "I know about as much about California as I do Texas. I've never been there, either."

"But I thought all Americans went to Hollywood to, you know, see the movie stars and to surf," Tatyana said.

"You don't have to go to California to surf," I said. "We have an ocean on the East Coast, too."

"Do you have any movie stars?" she asked.

"Not really," I said, thinking about it. "Denzel Washington came to town once, when the movie Remember the Titans came out. But I didn't see him."

"You've never met Drew Barrymore, or Orlando Bloom, or ANYONE?" she asked.

"The President came to my school once," I said.

"Oh," she said, clearly disappointed.

"Tatyana," I said, "even though California is in the U.S., it's like three thousand miles away from where I live. Asking me if I've been there is like asking you if you've been to South Africa."

"I've been to South Africa," she said.

"Or Korea," I said.

"I've been to Korea," she said.

I was going to ask her about Malaysia next, but instead— feeling very unworldly—I decided to shut up.

Lahn, then, started saying something in French. I didn't know why he thought either of us would know what he was saying, until Tatyana said something back to him, also in French.

Feeling unworldly AND uncultured now, I listened to them talk for a while. I didn't understand any of it except these three words: "Drew," "Barrymore," and "Hollywood."

"Lahn has seen Drew Barrymore in person!" Tatyana told me, excitedly. "In Hollywood!"

"Huh," I said.

Lahn and Tatyana had another little conversation then. This time I could understand only THESE words: "geeky" and "jock."

(AGAIN, thank you SO much, Delia.)

Pushing my left hand under my leg, I pointed to Noori and AJ who were (thankfully) arriving. "Look! Our drinks!"

"Lahn was wondering why it says 'geeky jock' on your hand," Tatyana said to me, apparently not falling for my attempt at diversion.

"Oh, really?" I responded. "And you told him . . ."

"I told him it means you're smart and strong," she said.

Feeling a little better (and hoping she HAD said that, but how would I know?), I got up and jumped into the pool. I almost drowned when my T-shirt covered my nose and mouth, but after that it was fun.

Noori got in the pool, too, and we pretended we were mermaids by swimming with our feet together. At some point—just when we were getting bored, luckily—Gilligan got on the DJ's microphone, and told everyone it was time for the "BIG SURPRISE!" We were going to "MIX IT UP!" He told us to go around and find "SOMEONE SPECIAL!" with a matching wristband, and "HEAD TO THE DANCE FLOOR!"

"This should be entertaining," I said, floating on my back and watching the crowd. Predictably, the "it-girls" (there are at least ten Britney Spears look-alikes on this boat, I SWEAR) immediately began shrieking and running after all the guys, checking out their wristbands. The "cool" kids (in their sunglasses, even though it's night) acted as if they hadn't heard anything Gilligan said (which is a real possibility, actually). Then the gamers got all activated when one boy yelled, "TOURNAMENT!" and flung his wristband at the sea god statue, just catching one of the teeth of the trident and starting a tidal wave of wristband-flinging.

"Blue," Noori, who was standing in the water next to me, said. "AJ's got blue—just my luck. I've got orange."

I noticed, then, that AJ was at the edge of the pool holding his arm up and pointing at his wristband. "What color do you have, Brady?" he was calling out.

"Yeah, just MY luck, too—I've got blue," I said, thinking it might be time to FIRE my favorite color for betraying me in this way.

But THEN, thinking quickly (as, of course, I'm known to do), I grabbed Noori's hand underwater, did a little switcheroo, and—TA DA!—I pulled my arm out of the water and pointed at MY wrist, which now sported an ORANGE wristband.

"NOORI HAS BLUE!" I called out to AJ.

And before he could react, Noori was out of the water and pulling him off to the dance floor through the spray of flying wristbands.

(I'm sorry for doubting you, Color Blue. You remain my fave.)

Uh-oh. I guess I lost track of time. Mi madre is standing at the door of the cabin, CLAPPING at me to get up.

Maybe encouraging her to be our tour guide was a bad idea. The power seems to have gone to her head.

Adios—

Brady

Dear Delia,

Now I will tell you about my day in Barcelona. And I'm going to do it at the same speed my Nazi tour guide—er, mother—set for the day. I think reading it will be sort of like that day in class when we read those Faulkner stories, which had these whole long paragraphs that were just one sentence, and we read them real fast and tried to only take a breath after each period. Well, it's like that, only worse. So, take a very deep breath to start and GO!

The first thing we saw was a statue of Columbus, which had a sign in front of it that said (and I'm not making this up, although I could be leaving out an accent mark, but what-ev) "COLON," causing me to wonder if the Spaniards know that word means "intestine," which doesn't seem like a very flattering thing to call a person, seeing how it's a bodily organ that's filled with, uh . . . well, you know what it's filled with; but I couldn't ponder that for long, because my arm was in sudden danger of being separated from the rest of my body since my mother was "guiding" me to the Gothic Quarter, which is a super old and stony place, where we stood in the very spot Queen Isabel stood when she greeted Columbus upon his return to Spain after his famous discovery of our continent (although some years later it was proved that he was actually full of crap, and never made it to America at all, which—now that I think about it—might have something to do with that sign in front of the statue . . .).

(You can breathe in now.)

Then we went into a shop where someone who looked like a Native American (perhaps they are called Native Spaniards in Spain) was selling silver and turquoise jewelry, hippie clothing, incense, and pot pipes, so my mother pulled me out of that shop quickly due to an infiltration of inappropriateness into her carefully planned itinerary, and we went back to the busy street where we looked for a place my mother's guidebook recommended for authentic Barcelonese snack foods, but since we couldn't find it after marching around in the blazing sun for at least two or three minutes, I pulled my mother into the door of McDonald's, where we ate McPitas.

(Breathe now!)

Then, we (that means my mother) studied the subway map, and we (that means my mother) decided to take the subway to Parc Guelle, a place that has artsy statues and stuff done by a local artist named Gaudi, who designed bunches of buildings in Barcelona and lived at some other time that my mother told me all about as we rode the subway, which might have interested me if I weren't sleep-deprived, having been at the Roman Ruins party and walking around the boat until midnight.

(Breathe . . .)

After we arrived at the subway station, which my mother swore (take note of this) was the nearest to Parc Guelle, we stood on a street corner and saw no park anywhere, so we went into a shop where my mother reached back into the ancient recesses of her brain for some Spanish phrases she learned in the seventh grade, and (miraculously) began emitting Spanish words in the direction of this man, who looked at her quizzically (since, as it turns out, many Spanish people don't speak Spanish, but something called Catalon), until she finally shrugged and said, "Parc Guelle?" to which the man smiled and pointed to his right, then up to the sky.

(YES! Breathe!)

Following his detailed instructions, we set out to the right and immediately came to understand his "up" direction, because there was an extremely steep and long sidewalk/stairway with an escalator running up the middle of it, going so high into the sky that the top was obscured by a mist, and we began going up, not knowing if it were the stairway to Parc Guelle or the stairway to heaven, my mother on the stairs and I on the escalator for the first half-hour, after which we stopped for a break at one of the cafés that lined this stairway, then continued our journey (my mother taking the escalator, too, at this point), until we reached a sign at the edge of a little wooded path, which read: Parc Guelle.

(If you have not already hyperventilated, breathe . . .)

After mustering our strength for a few lame cheers, we trotted past the sign—which turned out to be a LIE—and hiked along this path covered with roots (which at first I cursed because I kept tripping on them, but later worshipped because they served as a means of holding onto the earth as the hill increased to something close to a 90° angle), until we rounded a bend in the path and could hear the sounds of music in the distance, which I hoped would not turn out to be harps played by angels.

(Breathe . . .)

Parc Guelle was really cool, with these awesome, long walls (purposely wavy, and not—as I first thought—a sign that I was delirious) made from tiny, colorful tiles, going around this whole huge plaza (placa, I believe, in Barcelonese) from which you could see the entire city below—easily a million miles away—so we slumped onto a bench and looked at the view, listened to the sounds of Spanish guitars from a stage below us, and then (after we recovered—perhaps a week later) we went to the other side of the park where there was a big lizard made from the same tiles and a gate leading out to a street, where we saw a sign pointing to a subway station, which turned out to be (hear this) just FOUR blocks away, over FLAT terrain.

(Okay, breathe.)

Once back on the subway, I closed my eyes and listened to my mother have this little discussion with herself (since I was no longer speaking to her), which seemed to be all about adjusting our itinerary to take into account that we had only made it to stop three out of fifteen, or something, and we were almost out of time, so when we arrived at our destination station she pulled on my arm (to wake me up) and asked me which one of these I wanted to do: see some Gaudi architecture, visit a reptile museum, or buy some clothes.

(Breathe . . .)

I really wanted to go to the reptile museum (HA HA HA), but instead figured I would be practical and pick out something new to wear tonight on the boat, since it is a "dress up" night, so my mother suggested we look for some local Spanish fashions, but all of the shops seemed to carry only clothes from Paris, so I ended up with a GREAT denim skirt with little blue seed-beads sewn in designs all over it, and then I thanked my mother (since I was speaking to her again—the clothing purchase having worked well to re-open mother-daughter communication lines), and we ran all the way back to the statue of Christopher Colon and up the gangplank of our boat just as the whistle blew, informing us we were leaving port.

(Okay, you MADE it! Unless, of course, you are on the floor, dead.)

As you can see, being a tourist in Barcelona is exhausting. It also builds an appetite, so, luckily, we went right to the dining room when we got on the boat. I had two lobster tails at dinner. It was all-you-can-eat, and I was actually going to have three, but Cristo the waiter moves so slowly that he didn't quite make it to the table with the third plate before Mom made me run up to deck ten to see the sunset. Which was really awesome. Think big red, uh, marshmallow melting into deep blue, uh, cocoa. As you can tell, I am still hungry. Which is okay, since there is a death-by-chocolate party in the teen lounge in about an hour. Delia, I truly think we should consider becoming stowaways on a cruise ship. Life is very good here. That is, if you never leave the boat.

Now . . . where WAS I in the "Poseidon's Mixer" story before I was (so RUDELY) interrupted by Barcelona? Think . . . think . . . think . . . oh, yeah! I was in the pool, and Noori had just dragged AJ to the dance floor . . .

"Brady! Hurry, let's go!" Tatyana called to me.

"Without Noori?" I asked.

"We'll improve her chances of snagging him if we leave," she said. "Trust me."

"Where are we going?" I asked, pulling myself out of the pool.

"The Internet Café?" she suggested. "I told my grandfather I'd e-mail him. He's 85 years old—and a MAJOR Web freak."

"He should meet my sister," I said, drying my legs with a towel. "Can I go like this? I'm totally soaked."

"Just take off the shirt," she said. "You'll dry a lot faster that way."

"Uh, that's okay, I'm all right," I said, looking around at all the people, and then at Lahn—who MIGHT have been looking at me, because he quickly averted his eyes.

"You're modest, aren't you?" Tatyana said. "THAT'S why your friend wrote that thing on your hand about wearing a bikini, isn't it? Well, Brady, you should JUST DO IT. Isn't that what jocks say? And—trust me—you'll have WAY more thrilling adventures and attract WAY more Euro-hotties if you WEAR the bikini. In PUBLIC."

I thought about you, then, Delia, and how AMAZING it is that I SOMEHOW attracted a new friend SO much like YOU.

And I asked myself this question: WHEN will my life stop being so HUMILIATING?

"Hey!" some girls said to me as they walked by. "You're the one we were looking for all over the boat last night—the one who choked!"

The answer to my question: Apparently not SOON.

Trying to ignore all that had occurred in my life up to that moment, I threw a towel over my shoulders and followed Tatyana.

On our way out, we passed Gilligan, who was trying to stop the wristband tournament that was well underway at one end of the pool. There were several wristbands on each of the trident's teeth and dozens floating on the surface of the water.

"Now, now," he was saying to a girl who was getting into the pool to retrieve a wristband that had apparently missed its mark. "Let's not throw things at King Poseidon, please."

"Okay, sorry about that," the girl said to him. "But isn't that statue supposed to be Neptune?"

That, of course, was very amusing to us, so we laughed our way down the elevator and all the way into the Internet Café. People looked at us like we were weirdos, which was also amusing.

Doing some quick calculations, I realized that it was afternoon in the US, so I checked to see if anyone was online. I only found one person I knew, though. Guess who? You're RIGHT—Clare! Two points! My IM conversation with her was yet another source of amusement for Tatyana and me, so I printed it out so YOU, TOO, can be entertained . . .

allgutsallgirl: Clare! Is that you?

ferretlover: diku?

allgutsallgirl: What does that mean?

ferretlover: do I know u?

allgutsallgirl: I think. I'm your sister. Brady.

ferretlover: o. uv nevr imd me b4. r u @ delias?

allgutsallgirl: Uh, no, I'm in Europe.

ferretlover: lol.

allgutsallgirl: I'm serious, Clare. I've been gone for days.

ferretlover: duz mom no?

allgutsallgirl: She's with me.

ferretlover: tht xplns it.

allgutsallgirl: That explains what?

ferretlover: y i havnt cn her 18ly.

allgutsallgirl: Riiiight. So, how are you?

ferretlover: ssdd.

allgutsallgirl: Which means . . .

ferretlover: same stuff, different day.

allgutsallgirl: That's descriptive. How's Irene?

ferretlover: she's bin goin 2 a day camp.

allgutsallgirl: Irene NEVER goes to camp.

ferretlover: o.

allgutsallgirl: What kind of camp is it?

ferretlover: idk.

allgutsallgirl: Huh?

ferretlover: i don't know. bbiam.

allgutsallgirl: Clare, I HATE chatspeak.

ferretlover: be bak in a minit. askin dad.

allgutsallgirl: ladeda ladeda ladeda ladeda ladeda ladeda ladeda ladeda ladeda ladeda ladeda ladeda ladeda ladeda la

ferretlover: field hockey.

allgutsallgirl: WHAT??!!?

ferretlover: i speld thoz wrds out.

allgutsallgirl: I read it, but I don't GET it. Irene has never done a sport in her entire LIFE. She was out of PE for a whole year, once, for a ping-pong injury.

ferretlover: wow.

allgutsallgirl: Does that mean something other than "wow"?

ferretlover: no, jst wow. she's a goalie.

allgutsallgirl: A GOALIE! Have you ever seen all the gear field hockey goalies wear? They look like enormous marshmallows.

ferretlover: i no! lol. she keeps it on wen she gets home, n she slept in it last nite. stik n all.

allgutsallgirl: Oh, oh, oh, oh, oh. I get it now.

ferretlover: get wut?

allgutsallgirl: The snake's still loose.

ferretlover: wut snake?

allgutsallgirl: I've got to go, Clare. I think the ship is sinking or something.

ferretlover: wut ship?

allgutsallgirl: Bye, Clare! Kiss-kiss!

ferretlover: kiss means keep it simple stupid.

allgutsallgirl: Ooops—sorry. But I bet Freud would have something to say about that.

ferretlover: who?

allgutsallgirl: Love you! Give Dad and Irene hugs for me!

So, after that intellectually stimulating conversation, and after Tatyana wrote a long e-mail to her granddad in Lebanon, we wandered out on the deck. There was a noisy crowd at one end, and it turned out to be a bunch of people from the party. Apparently, the evening tournament had shifted from ring-the-sea-god to shuffleboard. I wanted to play, but Tatyana dragged me to the other end of the boat to stargaze. Which turned out to be very illuminating (hehe), because THERE, standing at the rail—aglow in starshine, like Kate Winslet and Leonardo DiCaprio—were Noori and AJ. And they were in the middle of a MAJOR KISS. (And I don't mean "keep it simple, stupid.")

When I saw them, I thought: Noori must be a GREAT dancer. And then I felt an odd "pang." I wondered if it might be a raging hormone trying to confuse me about whether or not it was a good idea to let the nice Texas boy go. But, NO, it turned out to be Tatyana poking me in the ribs.

"Let's leave them alone," she mouthed, pulling me off to stargaze somewhere else.

Okay. You're all caught up on my adventures, and I've got to get ready to go. I have to figure out what top will go with my new skirt. (And, no, I WON'T pick a shirt with any numbers on it—I KNOW how to dress up, Delia. I think.)

I need to take a shower, too, which is something I'm not looking forward to. Delia, you would NOT BELIEVE how small the shower stall is. I swear it's no more than ten inches square. I'm TOTALLY afraid of getting stuck in it.

(Oh, BE quiet.)

Brady

Dear Delia,

We are now in the French Riviera, my extremely jealous friend. And, believe it or not, I am wearing the bikini with NO shirt over it! Aren't you IMPRESSED?

Okay, I haven't left my stateroom, but it's still a BIG step for me, because I'm so self-conscious about all this that I feel exposed even with no humans around. Or my mother, for that matter, who is in the shower preparing for another day ashore. I asked her if we could PLEASE hang out on the boat longer this morning, but she's not having it. I could hide out on the power-walking deck, but I'm too exhausted to slog my way up there.

It's not just Barcelona that has me worn out. It's also the party last night, which, basically, went on until 1:30 in the morning. Everyone was pretty hyper from the chocolate, I guess. There was a scale model of the cruise ship in white chocolate, anchored in a sea of dark chocolate. I am personally responsible for eating three chocolate deck chairs and two chocolate life jackets. Lahn ate an entire smokestack, Tatyana and Noori did in the chocolate hot tub, and AJ snarfed down all of deck nine, I think.

After that, Noori and AJ (who are still wearing their blue wristbands and STILL into PDAs, let me tell you) disappeared, and we only ran into them one other time during the party. It was at the beginning of Gilligan's "Treasure of the Sea Hunt," which was—as you can probably guess—incredibly dumb. He was ALL EXCITED about it, though, and had written little clues, but after about a minute of explaining the rules to everyone over the speakers in the lounge, one of the gamers yelled, "TOURNAMENT!" and EVERYONE shot over to the foosball tables again. Gilligan was left standing there, all pathetic-like, so we took one of his clues and went off on the little treasure hunt (like complete dorks).

Tatyana read out the first clue: "Go to the place where the ceiling is space and look under the chair that is covered with hair."

We decided to go to deck ten—since that's the top of the boat—which turned out to be right, since we are so smart (and the clue was so stupid). There, we walked around the deck until we found a fur blanket (I hope faux) over one of the lounge chairs. And that's where we ran into Noori and AJ. They had crawled under it. (The blanket, not the chair.) Tatyana and I tiptoed away, while Lahn pulled a piece of paper out from under the leg of the chair. When we got about a half-deck away, Lahn opened it and seemed to be reading it, then said something to Tatyana in French.

"Lahn thinks the next clue is at the Roman Ruins Pool, because this clue says, 'Where the Romans fell, find a bell.'"

"Lahn read that?" I asked. "I thought he didn't know English."

He shrugged, then said something to Tatyana again.

"He says he knows English, but doesn't like speaking it because he thinks his accent isn't good," she said.

"So, he's understood everything we've said?" I asked.

Tatyana nodded.

"Like, at the pool party, when you were telling me how I would attract Euro-hotties if I wore my bikini?" I asked.

Tatyana nodded.

Lahn seemed to take up stargazing at that moment.

In an effort to shift the orbit of the conversation JUST a bit, I said to Tatyana, "Okay, wow! That's COOL that he can speak two languages—and YOU know three! You guys are awesome."

Lahn said something else in French, and Tatyana turned to me and said, "He knows Vietnamese, too."

"Oh," I said, nodding (in that whole-body sort of way).

"And, actually, I know four languages," she said, looking at me kindly.

(It's embarrassing being with these people. I wish you were here, Delia, because you are so simple.)

At the Roman Ruins Pool, the "bell" was not immediately apparent, so we divided the area into three sections and split up. I was given the pool itself, but since I was fully dressed, I couldn't exactly jump in to look for anything. So I walked slowly around the edge, gazing through the water. There were just a few people swimming, so I quickly determined there was no bell at the bottom of the pool. You may remember, though, that there is a statue of Neptune/Poseidon in the middle of this pool, and

THAT is where I spied the bell—a copper cow bell at the base of the statue.

This presented a problem, since there was no way to the statue except through the water. There was, however, a guy treading water very near the statue, so I figured I'd just call out to him and ask him to look under the bell and bring the clue to me. The guy was blond. Very blond—like a Swedish person. He also appeared to be very CUTE. So, of course, thinking I might have inadvertently stumbled upon a Euro-hottie, I took the opportunity to: PANIC.

Luckily (or so I thought), Tatyana appeared at that moment, and I pointed out the bell and the potential Euro-hottie and asked her to please communicate with him for me. She took the opportunity to: Tell me to FORGET IT.

"This could be your code-red Euro-hottie, Brady," she said. "Just do it."

I stood there, just doing nothing.

"Or I'll push you in the water," she added.

(Delia, did you SEND this person to me?)

Since I had chosen a white top to wear with my skirt and didn't want to look like I had participated in a wet T-shirt contest, I thought it best to do as I was told.

"Hello there!" I called out.

No response.

"Maybe he has earplugs in," she said.

"HELLO THERE!" I said, louder.

Slowly, he moved his head in our direction, but still didn't say anything.

"Do you speak English?" I called out.

He swam a little closer to us, but still didn't answer.

"Whoa," Tatyana whispered in my ear. "He is REALLY cute."

"Swedish?" I called out.

He shook his head and swam to the edge, right where we were standing.

"German?" I asked.

"No," he said, pulling himself out of the water at my feet.

"Uh, so, uh, then, uh, you, uh—" I said. (Very eloquently, don't you think?)

"I am Klingon," he announced.

Which was weird. But only slightly weirder than where he had positioned himself, which was VERY close and DIRECTLY in front of me, with his eyes fixed STRAIGHT ahead. And since—as it turns out—he is about eight inches shorter than I am, he was staring RIGHT at my, uh, basooma. I was afraid to move for fear of inadvertently knocking him back into the pool.

(This ISN'T funny, Delia.)

"Klingon?" Tatyana asked. "Is that in Europe?"

"Kling," he said, speaking directly into my shirt. "M-class planet, second in the Klingon Star System."

There was silence for a moment, during which time I hoped madly that Klingons are not possessed with X-ray vision. Then I took a careful step backward, but he just moved along with me.

"Aren't we REALLY late, Tatyana, for, you know, SOMETHING?" I asked.

Ignoring me, and apparently OBLIVIOUS to my mounting emergency situation, she said to him, "Is there a Klingon language?"

"Da pa pa pa go," he said, his head still not budging from its location in my frontage.

"Cool! What does that mean?" she asked.

"Targeting coordinates," he answered.

"Say something else," she said, obviously finding all this very entertaining.

"Sho pee-eh shuha."

"And that means . . . ," she said.

"Disengage cloaking device."

"Okay, 911!" I yelled, stepping in one direction and then another, TRYING to shed this guy who seemed STUCK to me by some invisible webbing device. FINALLY, I managed to free myself by—yes—FALLING in the pool.

(You are enjoying this, Delia, aren't you?)

He started to jump in after me, but I said, "STAY!" and you know what? He DID. And then he stood there at the edge of the pool, all lined up with Tatyana and Lahn (who had turned up at some point during all the commotion), LOOKING at me. I stood in the water, my Parisian skirt billowing around my legs, and my shirt filling with water.

"So, why are you so fixated on Brady, anyway?" Tatyana asked Klingon Boy as the three of them gazed down at me.

"She appears to be my type," he said.

"What type would that be?" she asked.

"Geek," he said.

(You will be SO DEAD when I get home.)

"She's not really a geek," Tatyana told him.

"THANK YOU," I said.

"What's your name?" Tatyana asked him.

"Gorkon," he said.

"Neat," she said. "And you say you're from another planet?"

I wondered: WHY is she encouraging him?

"He's a TREKKIE," I said.

She looked confused, and I realized—TOUCHÉ!—that I'd FINALLY found something I knew more about than she did. (Okay, it's a really DUMB thing, but I'll take it.)

"Star Trek—a TV show," I said. "There are people who are REALLY into it."

"I am lonely for Kling," Gorkon said.

"Oooh," Tatyana said, in an oh-poor-Gorkon sort of way. "Do you want to come with us on our treasure hunt?"

Then I wondered (while coughing very loudly): HAS SHE GONE COMPLETELY CRAZY?

"But you have to give Brady some distance, Gorky," she told him.

He nodded, mechanically, never looking up into Tatyana's face.

Then Lahn said something to Tatyana and pointed at the bell in the middle of the pool.

"And THAT'S how all this started," I said, swimming out to the statue and pulling a clue out from under the bell.

Lame clue #3 read: "Up and down it goes, at the bottom find a rose."

So we went on our merry way to the elevator, joined now by this new traveling mate we had picked up on our journey. I felt as if I had wandered onto the set of a REALLY BAD remake of The Wizard of Oz.

I would tell you the rest of the clues, but there were SO many of them, and they were SO idiotic that you'd probably throw yourself out the nearest open window if you had to read them all. Gorkon didn't stick with the hunt for very long—perhaps he needed charging—so there's nothing more to tell about him, either. So I'll just say that the clues eventually led us back to the teen lounge, where there were prizes waiting for us: CD cases. Very nice. And Gilligan had set out Twister boards, so we amused ourselves with those for a while.

(He DOES try.)

The shower has just turned off, which means ma mere (French, now—pronounced "mah mair," spoken through the nose) will be making me get up and go to Nice (pronounced neece). So THIS is IT! I'm DOING it! I'm WEARING THE BIKINI ON THE BEACH TODAY! And it's NOT to please YOU, it's to—well, actually it IS to please you. Oh, why aren't you here? This is going to be SO hard! I need an incentive to get out and do it. Like the threat of being beaten up by my best friend, for instance.

Hold on. My mother is saying something. It is, "We're behind schedule, let's go, Brady. And PUT something over the bikini top. It's inappropriate for walking around town."

All right, MOM! You DID it! The much needed incentive! A purpose for my bikini-wearing: rebellion! I'm obligated now, as a respectable teenager, to wear this bikini top in public ALL DAY, just to drive you CRAZY! I will proudly get up now and SALUTE my commanding officer! SIR!

Au revoir! (Pronounced o-vwah, and I hope you know what it means, because everyone else in the world does.)

Brady

Wednesday, before dinner
(The system of time here is based on floor mats
and food, as best as I can tell.)

Dear Delia,

I was BOLD today. I walked around the streets of Nice in my bikini top, and whenever I started to feel self-conscious—which was only every five seconds—I glanced over at ma mere, who then frowned at me—bless her—giving me the much-needed boost of self-confidence.

Sometimes parents really DO come through for you, I guess.

In my bikini top I ate glacé (that's ice cream in French, pronounced almost like "glass," which is a little frightening), shopped in little French shops and bought a blouse for you (which I think will fit you because I couldn't get the buttons to meet at all when I tried it on), and sat openly on benches in parks with French flags waving around me. I was liberated and happy! And then we went down to the shore.

There are many strange things about the beach in Nice. For instance:

- There is no sand. The beach is covered with egg-shaped rocks. I was lurching around as if one leg were eight inches shorter than the other.
- You can't lie down on a towel because of these rocks, so everyone sits up or stands, or (if it's not their first time there) they have beach chairs.
- There are these French guys on the beach who go around with coolers, selling actual HEALTHY snacks, like watermelon slices and oranges. It's MADNESS!
- And, the last—and MOST—strange thing about the beach in Nice: It's a topless beach.

Imagine my surprise when I stepped (well, hobbled) onto the crowded beach, my head and my, uh, bikini top held high, and then gazed around at all these other females sunbathing and swimming, all looking as if they had been dressed by the tailor from THE EMPEROR'S NEW CLOTHES. And it was all KINDS of people, Delia—whole families were boinging and flapping in the Mediterranean breezes! People with little tops, big tops, old tops, and young tops. (Did Dr. Seuss write that? Oh, no, that was fish.)

"How did I miss THIS in the descriptions?" my mother said, her face turning DayGlo red. Standing there next to me and my blue bikini and white wrap, I'm thinking we represented our flag well. (Of course, the French flag is red, white, and blue, too, but WHATEVER.)

"Ma mere," I said, feeling it was my duty to tease her at that particular moment, "now I'm wondering about the term 'inappropriate' in THIS situation. Isn't it 'inappropriate' when you sort of do something that ISN'T expected of you? So when you're at a topless beach, aren't you sort of EXPECTED to go around topless? You know, like, isn't it 'inappropriate' to WEAR a top?" I asked, reaching behind me, pretending to look for the clasp of my bikini.

"Brady," my mother said in a don't-even-think-about-it tone, "You're wearing me down enough today, so let's not—"

At which point she was interrupted by a very loud scream that came from my mouth when my bikini top FLEW OFF, as if flung from a slingshot. Panicking, I threw my arms across my chest and looked over at my mother, who was just STANDING there, looking really MAD, her arms on HER chest (which, unlike mine, was covered with a swimsuit—a nice, simple, racing-style swimsuit—like the one I USED to have—when my life was SIMPLER and my best friend didn't FORCE me to buy clothing that likes to FLY off my body).

Frantically, I started to root around amongst the rocks with one arm (with the other I was trying to keep myself covered up, but I SWEAR my arm has gotten smaller lately—oh, SHUT UP), but the top was being kicked around by a parade of French feet, so I struggled there for HOURS (okay, maybe twenty seconds . . . but a really LONG twenty seconds) when suddenly a woman appeared in front of me, my bikini top in her hand. She was ninety years old, or maybe a hundred, and abundantly cheery and obviously very helpful. Like a fairy godmother. In a swimsuit. SANS TOP.

(In case there is any question in your mind, Delia, "sans" is French for "without." I want to make sure you can accurately picture the situation I was in, but for your own well-being, I recommend you DON'T.)

The woman held my bikini top out to me, but my brain must have thought it was a stun-wand, because I immediately became paralyzed. I tried desperately to make my mouth utter some expression of thanks, but NOTHING would come out. This didn't seem to bother the woman, though. She kindly placed the bikini top in my hand and then vanished with an "au revoir!" And I put the thing back on—with no help from ma mere, thankyouverymuch.

I think she still believes I popped that thing off on purpose. I mean, WHO WOULD DO THAT? Okay, maybe all those people on that beach, but who ELSE would do that?

You know, Delia, even though I have been made—once again—to feel like an idiot in front of all humanity, I am STILL proud of myself today. I WORE the bikini, Delia! In PUBLIC! And, now, back on the boat, I am basking in the sun at the pool—á la bikini—and I'm not even slightly self-conscious. (OK. Slightly. But that's all right.) I just went for a swim and was actually able to get up some speed this time, since I no longer had a T-shirt strangling me during the freestyle.

"I've thought about what happened today, Brady," ma mere is saying to me at this moment. She has been at the boat's shops for the last hour and is now standing next to my lounge chair.

"I guess it doesn't make sense that you would do that on purpose. And you did seem awfully surprised. Must have been a loose clasp."

"Yes, obviously a defective part," I am saying. "I think there may be a lawsuit in this."

Ignoring my very funny comment, she is now saying: "I was just kind of peeved about you wearing that bikini top in town. I mean, I know it took you a long while to feel comfortable wearing it at all . . ."

"Uh, do we have to talk about this?" I am interjecting. (Love my mom and all, but some conversations are clearly for friends only.)

". . . and I know you were feeling some pressure about all that," she's now saying, nodding toward my hand (as in, the WRITING on it).

"That's right, yes, of course, it's all Delia's fault," I have just told her (in a very enjoyable way). "So, now can we stop talking about this?"

"Okay," she says as she takes her pool wrap off and drops into the lounge chair next to———

Oh. MY. <u>GOD</u>!

SHE IS WEARING A <u>BIKINI</u>!

"MOM," I whisper frantically, "when did you get THAT?"

"Just now," she says nonchalantly.

"Don't you, uh, think that's sort of, uh, kind of, uh—"

"Inappropriate? I think the pool is the right place for a bikini, don't you?" she says.

"But, uh," I sputter, "you NEVER, uh . . ."

"I used to wear bikinis, Brady. I grew up in the seventies. But I haven't worn one since Irene was born. I was bothered about weight gain and stretch marks."

Uh, TOO MUCH INFORMATION, I am thinking.

"But, you know what, Brady? Today—this whole trip, actually—has changed me. Seeing how the Europeans are so free with their bodies, well, it has made me feel emboldened."

My mother is emboldened.

Be scared.

Be VERY scared.

To complete the picture of what is rapidly becoming a typical sort of afternoon in my life, Gorkon has now appeared by my chair.

"Who is your friend?" he is asking.

I look around for a second and then realize he is talking about my mother.

"That is my mother," I am saying to him. Then, whispering, I add: "She's a geek."

I think I'll go swim a few more laps.

Oy!!!

Brady

Thursday
(No, wait! That can't be right! We go home
on Friday, and I'm not ready!!)

Dear Delia,

We are pulling into a new port—Livorno, Italy.

Hm. Does a cruise ship "pull in"? I don't think so. A cruise ship "arrives," I guess. Well, whatever it does, we're doing it.

Livorno is a very industrial-looking place with lots of big, rusty ships and factories and stuff. This is not the place where we are spending the day, though. We're taking a train to Florence. Or Firenza, which is apparently the Italian name for it.

Mio madre (note I'm back to Italian) woke up really early and headed to the Internet Café to do research for our day in Florence. She spent some time there last night, too, by the way. I suspect she is trying to avoid surprises, such as the one we encountered on the beach in Nice. Or else, in her emboldened state, she was making plans to jump ship and run off to become a tour operator in the Mediterranean. Nothing would surprise me anymore, after the mother-in-a-bikini occurrence.

Per usual, she wants to get going as soon as we are allowed to get off the boat, because she says the trip to Florence is over an hour, and then we'll have exactly three hours there, and then we'll get on a train to Pisa, where she says we'll run to the Leaning Tower and take a picture, and then we'll run back to the train and arrive back in Livorno with just enough time to get on board before the boat leaves port. Feeling a case of Barcelona coming on, and worrying about such a tight schedule, I asked my mother what we're supposed to do if one of our trains is late and we miss the boat. She just waved her hand at me and sort of tutted. As you can see, having an emboldened mother can be very risky business.

This morning I e-mailed my little sister. My mother kept bugging me about doing that, even though I TOLD her Clare and I have already had a VERY deep and meaningful

IM conversation this week. But choosing not to start an argument (SOMEONE has to get sensible), I went ahead and did it. Here is what I wrote:

Dear Clare,

Yesterday I was in the French Riviera. The shopping was excellent! Apparently, there is some law about clothing sales in France, and because of this they have sales only two months out of each year. And guess what? One of the months is JULY! (Which is this month, in case you are having a hard time keeping a check on reality in my absence.) By the way, our mother has become an exhibitionist. If you don't know what that means, ask Jeeves.

Brady

p.s. Please give the following note to Irene

Dear Irene,

Even though I've always refused, on principle, to participate in sports that require athletes to wear skirts and ribbons, I may reconsider in regard to field hockey, since you have recently taken it up. Goalie, huh? That's AWESOME. I guess that's one way to become the big one.

Yesterday I spent the day in Nice. It was amazing. I sat and watched the rolling, white waves glisten in the Mediterranean sun, my view only occasionally obscured by big, bouncing—

Your loving sister,
Brady

After I took care of that task, I headed to the breakfast buffet and pigged out. Literally. I ate bacon. Plus pancakes, and French toast, and eggs, and a mocha latte. If everyone on this boat is eating as much as I am, we will surely sink before the end of this cruise.

Seriously, though, I am getting SO out of shape. I feel like the Super Size guy in that movie. (SHUT. UP.) Not only am I snarfing down WAY too much food, I have TOTALLY gotten out of my running routine, what with my mother's sightseeing schedule (which is a workout, for sure, but more mental than physical) and the constant demands of my cruise-ship social circle (a.k.a. the Odd Squad, as I am now calling us since Gorkon beamed himself down to join in).

Speaking of which, I ran into Tatyana and Noori at breakfast. They told me they are staying on the boat today.

"We've been to Florence, like, five times," Tatyana said. "So we're going to get facials, do the fitness room, sunbathe, drink virgin piña coladas. Stuff like that."

Which sounded REALLY good, actually. I mean, I WANT to see Florence, of course, but I started thinking how, if I stayed, I could get in a five-mile run, do some serious lap-swimming while the pool isn't so crowded, drink a few of those virgin piña coladas, AND take a nap. (The last two items being #1 and #2 on my brain's priority list, I'm embarrassed to say. Welcome to blob world.) I started to think about approaching my mother with the request, when Tatyana said:

"I know what you're thinking, but you HAVE to go to Florence, Brady." And she poked her finger at my hand (which was, at that moment, very busy shoveling a fifth piece of bacon into my mouth), and specifically at that #4 instruction (which just WON'T fade away).

Before I could respond, Gorkon wandered up to us.

Truthfully, it's a mystery that he ever figures out where we are. His head is always in straight-ahead-robot mode, and his eyes never venture anywhere NEAR our faces.

"Remember, Gorky, Brady needs SPACE," Noori said, when he'd planted himself a little too close to me again.

"Space," he said, not moving a muscle. "The final frontier."

Tatyana gently pulled him back a few steps. "Brady doesn't really want you there in HER frontier, Gorky," she said.

(Clever, isn't she, Delia? I will NEVER let you two meet.)

"AS I was saying, Brady," Tatyana continued, poking at the word "Euro-hottie" on my hand again. "TODAY is your last chance."

"Brady," Gorkon said, "do you hurl heavy objects?"

I was grateful for this question. It represented a change of subject. "Yeah, sure!" I said. "Why?"

Smiling, he answered, "Klingon women hurl heavy objects."

Quickly realizing I'd made a bad move, I turned my attention back to Tatyana. "I think I've proven I'm not very good at finding, uh, the #4 thing," I said, making discreet head motions in the direction of Gorkon.

"Klingon women roar when they hurl objects," he said.

"Oh, well, sorry, then," I said to him. "I'm not much at roaring."

"What do Klingon men do?" Noori asked him.

"They duck a lot," Gorkon said.

We laughed at that for a while—including Gorkon, but I'm about 100% sure he hadn't meant to be funny.

Mio madre has returned from the Internet Café with reams of printouts, and she is doing that clapping thing again. I'll write later, although it may be on postcards I scribble out between shifts at the factories in Livorno, where I'll likely be working to earn money for a plane ticket home when we miss the boat later today, which will make us miss our plane tomorrow. But, hey, I guess it would give me more time to meet a Euro-hottie.

Arrivederci . . .

Brady

Thursday evening

Dear Delia,

I am COMPLETELY BUMMED about tonight being my last night on this ship. Even though it's been less than a week, I feel strangely at HOME here. The stateroom may be the size of a walk-in closet, and the bed the size of an ironing board, but there you are.

There's a farewell party tonight, and I really should be taking a shower and figuring out what to wear. Of course, what to wear shouldn't be a huge deal, because all my tops are dirty except my "Alexandria Recycles" T-shirt. (Uh, why did I bring THAT?) The matter of taking a shower may be a little more difficult, though, because our porter has shaped my bath towel into a rabbit tonight. Very cute, but I'm feeling squeamish about taking a furry animal apart. So, I will instead take the time to write you now, since you are probably patiently (HA HA HA) waiting for the report of my day in Florence and my pursuit of the Euro-hottie.

Mio madre and I took a bus to the Livorno train station, which I am guessing took longer than she had scheduled for in her carefully planned itinerary, because when it arrived, she felt the need to grab my hand and RUN at top speed. The train station was buzzing with Italian life, much of it male, so I began doing some hottie hunting right off, which ended abruptly when my mother stopped short in front of a vending machine, causing me to run into her with such force that I almost flipped over her head like a circus performer.

"This is the place to buy tickets," I could hear my mother's voice saying through the dizzying chirps of cartoon birds around her head. "According to Rick Steves, people in these stations don't always speak English, so it is best to use these machines."

I was curious about this but didn't dare ask any questions for fear of having to hear the (potentially boring and long) answers. The things I wondered: Who is Rick Steves, and is he the Euro-hottie I'm looking for? AND, why is an Italian vending machine easier to communicate with than an Italian human, and should I be worried about that?

The answer to one of those questions (you decide which) became clear when a screen appeared on the vending machine with a menu of language choices—French, English, Japanese, etc. As a cute little joke, I reached out to press "Greek," but I changed my mind when I noticed my mother's hand ready to violently slap mine away from the machine.

(The lesson I have learned: Never get in the way of a mother-turned-emboldened-tour-guide.)

On the train, we sat next to—get this!—an Italian man. (No, not Euro-hottie material, but cute in a unibrow-ish sort of way.) Mom thought this was a "marvelous opportunity" to practice our Italian, to which I replied, "Our what?" So she handed me a piece of paper, on which she had written out— just for me!—many Italian phrases with pronunciations and meanings. Here are a few she included on the list:

<u>prego</u> (PRAY-go)—please, you're welcome, all right

<u>e basta</u> (eh BAH stah)—that's enough

<u>per favore</u> (pair fa VOOR ay)—please

<u>il dolce far niente</u> (eel DOHL chay far nee EN tay)—the sweetness of doing nothing

"Why are there two words for 'please'?" I asked her.

"I guess you can use either," she said.

"And what about that 'il dolce far niente' thing?" I asked. "In what situation, exactly, would I say that?"

"I don't know," she said. "It's just so wonderful. I think the Italians would be impressed."

"And then they'd, uh, speak Italian to me?" I asked.

To this she nodded enthusiastically, obviously not seeing the inherent problem with convincing a population that you speak a language you actually don't.

I reached into my pack at that point for my Discman and CDs, facing the fact that it would be a VERY long trip to Florence.

"Prego," my mother said, turning to the Italian man next to her.

I wondered what she meant by this. Please? You're welcome? Maybe she was trying to be cool and was saying "All RIGHT!"

I watched to see if a high-five would follow. But, no. She began saying a bunch of words that made no sense to me (or probably anybody), and the Italian man nodded politely at her and glanced over at me. I smiled back at him, hoping my mother had not inadvertently offered me for sale.

Then the man said something which sounded very musical, somehow, and included the word "Firenza." My mother nodded, somewhat carefully. (I think "Firenza" was the only thing she understood, too.) Then the man went into this whole THING with lots of words ending in vowels, arm gestures, and nods of the head. I had an urge to applaud when he was done, but instead I just stared at him. My mother did the same.

Then he sighed, in an Italian sort of way, and began a pantomime with his briefcase, holding it tightly against his chest, and then moving it in the air. At the end of it all, he uttered what may be the only English word in his vocabulary: gypsies.

Mom leaned over to me and whispered, "I think he's warning us about the gypsies who attack tourists in Florence."

"Why are you whispering?" I asked her. "He obviously doesn't speak English." Then giving some thought to what she had actually SAID, I added, "WHAT gypsies who attack tourists?"

"I read about that online," she said, patting the man gently on his knee as he sighed, loudly, again. He was obviously very distressed about this gypsy thing.

I stared out the window at the sunflower fields going by in a blur, wondering what the Italian gypsies would be like. Joyful people in colorful, beaded clothes? Or more like those Irish boat people in the movie, <u>Chocolat</u>? Then (because I'm trying very hard to keep my promise to you, Delia) I wondered if any of the gypsies would be hotties, like, say, Johnny Depp, who even I agree is a blistering, radiant code-red. A Johnny Depp attack couldn't be so terrible, I thought, as I slipped my headphones on and chilled for the rest of the train ride.

I'm glad I had that chance to relax, because mio madre went right back into manic-mode the second the train stopped. The first place she (very literally) dragged me to was the San Lorenzo Market, which was, actually, AWESOME. We MUST go there, Delia—you would not believe the stuff! The leather jackets are amazing! I wanted to try them on, but before I had one off the hanger, Mom said we had to move on.

"Time to see David!" she said, over her shoulder.

"David?" I asked.

"Michelangelo's David!" she answered.

I glanced back at the leather coats of the San Lorenzo Market, all waving their sleeves at me (YES, they WERE), and then I followed my mother into the crowded street. She was jetting along so fast I could hardly keep up. At one point I lost her completely, but that was not my fault. It was YOUR fault, Delia. I was passing this crowd of teenage, back-packed boys who were speaking what might have been German (but what would I know?), and I stopped for just the briefest moment to scan the group for any signs of Euro-hottiness. When I looked ahead again, my mother was nowhere to be seen.

"This is NOT working," I said, aloud, to myself. (No, I don't know why.)

One of the German-ish boys looked over at me and said, "America?"

"Yes," I said, looking closely at him, sizing him up as a code-orange. If nice, I could easily bump him up to red, I thought. Which made the nervousness start rising, rising . . .

"Where?" he asked.

. . . rising, rising . . .

"Across the Atlantic Ocean," I said, knowing IMMEDI-ATELY that I was, well, an IDIOT. He wasn't asking me where America IS, of COURSE, but where I LIVE in America.

(Hottie hunting OBVIOUSLY has an adverse effect on IQ. Which might explain some things about YOU.)

He and all his friends started laughing at that, which avalanched him right into the Euro-glacier zone. I felt a sudden, crushing need to see my mother (which should give you some sense of the humiliation level).

I darted down the stone sidewalk, pushing my way through a large glom of people spilling off a bus, and found my mother standing on a street corner. She was scanning the crowds, and when she saw me, she signaled me over and said, "Come ON!"

"Aren't you even a LITTLE relieved to see me?" I asked, catching up to her roadrunner pace. "I could have been kidnapped by gypsies!"

"I don't think they KIDNAP people, Brady," she said. "What would they DO with a bunch of tourists? They probably just steal your money and go."

Then (CUE THE GYPSIES), a man dressed in a red suit appeared in my path and started entertaining us. He had a large water bottle balanced on top of his head and a dog that hopped on its back legs. (Uh, the dog wasn't on his head, in case I didn't make that clear.) Then, out of nowhere, two little kids—like, five years old or less, I swear—started bouncing around me, tugging at my backpack. My mother shooed them off and pulled me along.

Looking back at the red-suited man (who looked NOTH-ING like Johnny Depp, by the way), I said, "If those are the gypsies, I'm REALLY disappointed."

"We are SO behind," Mom complained, grabbing onto my hand, now, and shooting down the street.

"Mom," I whined, "slow down!" But she was completely oblivious.

Then, remembering the piece of paper in my jeans' pocket, I pulled it out and scanned her list of (seemingly useless) Italian phrases. "E-BASTA!" I yelled, grabbing onto a nearby lamppost. My arm almost came out of its socket, but it was worth it because she stopped.

I braced myself for the expected impatience of mother-turned-drill-sergeant, so IMAGINE my surprise when she SMILED at me. I had, apparently, impressed her with my command of the local language. "What, dear?" she asked.

"Mom," I said, panting (for dramatic effect). "I'm HUNGRY."

"But I planned on eating after the Uffizi," she said, pulling a piece of paper out of her pack.

"Uffizi?" I repeated. Whatever it was, it didn't sound very appetizing.

"Oh, no, not after the Uffizi," she said, looking over her notes. "We eat after we see David at the Academia. Can't you wait?"

"Uh, no," I said. "Let's get some take-out and we'll eat it, uh, on the steps of that big churchy-looking place over there."

"Oh, Brady!" she cried. "That's the Duomo!"

I wasn't sure if that was good or not, so I looked back down at my little cheat sheet and said, "Prego?"

She smiled at me again and said, "Okay."

(I'm DEFINITELY switching languages at school this fall. Italian apparently gives me complete mind control over my mother.)

We found some EXCELLENT pizza. Do you know that there are actual LAWS in Italy about what ingredients are allowed on pizza? In fact, they take pizza so seriously in this country that the colors on the FLAG are even about pizza. Madre told me this stuff—she said she learned it from the Internet. You know, in these Mediterranean lands, there are laws about pizza and clothing sales, but it's okay for women to go around with no shirts on. Interesting priorities.

Munching away on our pizza, we settled on the steps of the Duomo, and I asked Mom if I could see her list. It looked like this:

<u>THINGS TO DO IN FIRENZA</u>
San Lorenzo Market

Uffizi

Academia

Eat Italian food

Duomo

Ponte Vecchio

Piazza della Signoria

"Do you have a pen?" I asked my mother.

She handed me one, and I said, "So, what things on this list are museums?"

"The Academia and the Uffizi," she said enthusiastically.

I took the pen and made a line through those things.

"But—" Mom started to say.

"Mom, we go to the museums in Washington a LOT."

"But—"

"With the touring exhibits, I've probably even seen some of the things in these museums, right?"

"Oh, Brady, you've NEVER seen David," she said.

"DAVID, again," I said. "This guy is becoming an OBSESSION with you. I am SO telling Dad."

"It's a very important sculpture, Brady," she said (apparently not amused by, uh, me). She pulled her mammoth stack of papers from her pack and leafed through them until she found what she was looking for. "You know which one it is, right?"

I looked over her shoulder. "Oh, yeah, David. Very cute, in a naked-Bible-character sort of way."

"He's in the Academia, Brady," she said.

"Why don't we just go in THIS place?" I asked, looking up the steps to the doors of the Duomo. "It's on your list, and we're here."

She obviously liked that idea, so we went up the stone steps and through these huge doors, and into this mammoth, open room. It was dark, and old, and COLD. As we walked around, slowly, silently, I could feel the breath of the ancients on my neck and see the Renaissance artists hanging from the ceiling by their toes (or whatever they did), painting angels and clouds and stuff. Creepy, but I was INTO it. Until Mom broke the spell by saying, "Let's get information on the tours here."

"Tours?" I said. "Isn't that what we're DOING?" And then I hooked my arm into my mother's and headed for the side door.

"But—" she started saying again, but I kept pulling her out the door.

She suggested we stop and look at the map she'd gotten off MapQuest, but I assured her we didn't NEED a map, and we walked down some little street, which ended at a river. We stopped there and looked down at the gondolas—MOLTO Italiano.

"The Arno River!" she exclaimed.

"See? This method works perfectly. I lead you around—at a speed that doesn't break the sound barrier—and you tell me what we're looking at."

"And the Ponte Vecchio!" she cried even louder, pointing to a bridge that looked like a neighborhood block that had blown out in the river during a hurricane.

"It's even on your list!" I said (enthusiastically!).

"I was planning to walk through it, actually," she said.

"Uh, no," I said.

"But—" she said.

"Look, Mom," I said, deciding it was TIME. "I think it's AWESOME we're on this trip. You and Dad are REALLY

COOL for doing this for me, so don't get me wrong here. It's just that, a couple of times in the last few days—okay, LOTS of times in the last few days—I've thought that you're getting just a LITTLE too intense about this SIGHTSEEING thing. I mean, there might be some OTHER things I'd like to do, you know?"

She stared at me a sec with an okay-I'm-thinking-about-that sort of look on her face, and then the look changed to an okay-I'm-about-to-cry sort of look, and she said, "I'm so SORRY, Brady. I wasn't THINKING. I RUINED your trip!"

"Oh, no, Mom," I said (with an aren't-we-overreacting-a-bit sort of look).

"Yes I DID," she said, practically WEEPING. "We didn't do the things YOU wanted to do, and this is your special once-in-a-lifetime trip. I got SO into it, I guess because I'd never been to Europe before, or something, and I wanted everything to be PERFECT for you and something to remember, and—"

"MOM!" I said, taking her by the shoulders. "It's not that at ALL—I LOVE this trip. EVERYTHING about it."

"You do?" she asked, smiling through tears now.

(CLEARLY there was a PMS situation going on there.)

"Yes," I said.

"Then what is it?" she asked, wiping her eyes.

"I just want to go back to the San Lorenzo Market."

"Really?" she said, looking relieved.

I nodded and hooked my arm in hers again, and—practically skipping, like we were the stars of a REALLY sappy mother-daughter movie—we headed down the street and in pursuit of the San Lorenzo Market.

Soon we found ourselves in a long courtyard where all these performance artists were standing around being statues, like they do at the waterfront at home. There was this golden King Tut person and a white angel. Lots of people seemed to think they WERE statues, judging by their surprise when the statue-people moved after money was dropped in the boxes in front of them.

"Oh, Brady!" mio madre exclaimed. "Do you know where we ARE?"

I looked around—arches, stone buildings, a square of some sort ahead. "Florence?"

"The Uffizi!" Mom said. "I really think you'd like it, Brady—are you sure you don't want to go in?"

I looked at the long line of people baking in the sun in front of the gallery door and shook my head.

(I was enjoying my new job as tour-god. Oh, yes, I was.)

"Prego?" she asked, sweetly.

"Non, madre," I said, pulling her along toward the square.

"But—" she said, looking back at the line.

"We haven't bought Dad a gift yet," I pointed out.

"But—" she said, still looking back at the line.

"Or your other daughters," I added.

"But—"

"Mom," I said, still moving along with her in tow. "You're DOING it again. Do you have to be such a—"

That was when I noticed this ENORMOUS marble statue RIGHT next to us. I stopped, and looking up—in total awe—I said, "Big butt!"

Since she hadn't been looking ahead, she ran into me. Which must have pressed her reset button or something, because she switched into normal-mother-mode. Which is to say: She got mad.

"Brady!" she scolded. "It is SO inappropriate to call your mother a 'big butt.'"

"No, no, Mom," I said. "I wasn't calling YOU a big butt. I was calling THAT a big butt." And I pointed up to the back end of the statue, which was looming there, far above our heads.

"David," my mother said breathlessly—obviously so moved by the experience of gazing upon this gigantic rear end that tears started welling up in her eyes.

(Yes, DEFINITELY PMS happening today.)

"But I thought you said he was in a museum," I said.

"This is a reproduction," she told me. "The real one was here in this piazza until 1910 when it was moved to the Academia. The original was sculpted in 1504."

Impressed with my mother's knowledge of the period (or, at the very least, the regurgitation of what she learned in a David chat room), I asked, "Do you know why Michelangelo didn't give him any armor or anything? I mean, he's going to fight a giant, isn't he?"

"He has a slingshot," she said, pointing up at him. "And a rock."

"Oh, yeah, that would do it," I said.

"Amazing, isn't it?" She was in LOVE.

I almost said, "Mom, I find this REALLY INAPPROPRI-ATE for you to be SO enthralled with this humongoid marble dude and gazing up so longingly at all his giganto nakedness." But instead—catching myself, and getting suddenly FREAKED by the thought that maybe the mother-daughter movie we were actually in was one of those switched-body things—I began scanning the crowd to see if there was someone who looked uniquely American (that is, with a fanny pack) to ask directions to the San Lorenzo Market, since I not pnly didn't know WHO I was, I also didn't know WHERE I was.

That was when I noticed Lahn and his family in the crowd around David. "Lahn!" I called out. "Do you know the way to the San Lorenzo Market?"

Saying nothing to me—per usual—he pointed to the other end of the square, where I recognized something: the Duomo. We had made a circle, it seemed. I thanked Lahn and pulled my mother away from her, uh, colossal CRUSH and headed to the market.

I bought a mousepad (with David's torso on it) for Clare, a leather belt for Dad, and a sports watch for Irene. For myself, I found the PERFECT leather jacket. For once, I am looking forward to winter, because I can't WAIT to wear it. You can borrow it, but it probably won't fit since I bought the big one.

Shut up.

Mom spent the whole time looking at leather purses. Finally, she found one she really liked, and then put it back and said, "I shouldn't spend the money."

We did stop in Pisa on the way back, and we ran to the Leaning Tower, and someone took a picture of us standing in front of it. Then we ran back to the train station. I was thinking about how bizarre it is that people do that. I mean, there's nothing really to see in Pisa, except the tower, and people go just because it fell over by accident. I wonder if people would come from all over the world to see my house if it started teetering out into the street.

I've told you everything about the day, and, yes, as you have probably figured out, I failed in the Euro-hottie department. Unless you count one made of marble—David is definitely a hot-looking giant slayer. (Even IF my mother finds him attractive.)

Don't go nuts on me YET, though. It is still possible that I could strike code-red tonight at the party. After all, there are probably hundreds of guys on this boat, and I've only really met three of them. One doesn't talk (to me, at least), and the others are from weird, non-European places. So I think I'm due. Right?

I'm off to dismember a rabbit!

Brady

Friday, sometime during the day
(and that's about as close as I can get, because reality is
rapidly shifting as we fly back through time zones)

Dear Delia,

This plane is a whole lot more comfortable than that one we took over here last week. It's an Italian airline, and there's actually legroom, and the seats are bigger. Which makes no sense, since Americans are, by and large (no pun intended), bigger than Italians, so why do American airplanes have such skinny, teeny, tiny seats?

We even have a window seat this time. Mom and I decided that we would take turns sitting in it. I had the first four hours, which are up now, and I just switched with her. My mother is, at the moment, happily occupied with her headphones on, watching The Emperor's New Groove (and laughing out loud, occasionally, but I'm trying to ignore that), and the guy sitting to my right has been asleep this entire trip so far, with one of those airline sleep masks over his eyes. It's the perfect environment for writing my last letter to you.

Since we are on a daytime flight this time, I was able to see all kinds of cool things when we flew out of Rome this morning. The Mediterranean Sea looked like a painting from the plane—white ships on a dark blue canvas. We flew over the Alps, too, which are obviously some super-tall mountains, because there's mucho snow there, even in the middle of summer. The last piece of land I saw before we headed into the open Atlantic was the UK. (I waved to Georgia in England, forgiving her for the humiliation she caused—all's well that ends well, right? And anyway, WHAT would I read without her?)

My mother pointed out Ireland, which was a green dot in the sea. I thought about my ancestors again, and how they never saw this view of their homeland. It is so amazingly beautiful—a green I can't describe, Delia—and I felt this strong pull inside me, as if I were being called. I couldn't take my eyes off it as we passed over. We were so high up, and moving so fast by then, that a little plane far below us, moving in our same direction, looked as if it were flying backward. It was all VERY surreal.

When I could see only ocean from the window, I looked through my stuff from the San Lorenzo Market. I'd told Mom that I wanted to carry that bag on board because my luggage was too full, but it was really for a different reason. Mom and I looked, again, at the smooth belt and my jacket and talked about how great the leather is in Italy. Then I pulled the mousepad out.

"Are you sure that's an appropriate gift for Clare?" she asked. "I mean, it's so focused on, you know, David's, uh, middle ection."

"It's art, Mom," I said, dropping it back into the bag.

"Yeah, I guess that's right," she seemed to decide at that moment. "It's all pretty confusing, traveling in Europe, isn't it? They are so much freer about sexuality than we are in America."

Okay, WEIRD ZONE, I thought. My mother is trying to have a conversation with me about "sexuality." I pulled something else out of my bag to distract her. It was also the reason I was carrying the bag of gifts on the plane.

"Oh, Brady!" she said. "The purse!"

And she hugged me and told me I was so sweet, and she got all teary again, and I thanked her again for being such a great mom, and we hugged again, and etc., etc., and it was a happy (though really queer) ending to the trip, and I felt good because I had pleased her. I'm really glad this whole thing was such an enriching growth experience for her. (Even though I was the one who was supposed to grow and be enriched, I think, but WHATEVER.) Anyway, I am happy the purse pleased my mother.

These hours later, though—as we get incredibly close to the continent on which you are probably already headed to the airport to meet me—the question is this: Did I please my BEST FRIEND? Did I accomplish the LAST of your (insane) instructions, which I can STILL read on my hand. (I could do a COMMERCIAL for Sharpie pens.)

The answer, my friend, is in the story of . . .

THE HOTTIE HUNT

Which—believe it or not—was the actual theme of the farewell party last night. (I'm totally wondering if you somehow managed to IM Gilligan with this idea.) He gave us cameras, told us we had an hour to take a picture of our favorite "hotties" on the boat, and then he said he would print them out and hang them in the teen lounge before the end of the party. (Yay!!)

So, armed with a cam, the six of us—you know, the Odd Squad—set off on a hunting expedition. After about, say, three seconds, Noori took a picture of AJ, and AJ took a picture of Noori, and then they left. The rest of us were glad about this, actually, since they were being muy obnoxious—PDA-wise—on account of it being their last night together. Noori had actually been crying.

Down to four in our hunting party, we charged on through the jungle—er, cruise ship— and after about, say, ANOTHER three seconds, there was a surprise photo attack from someone ELSE in our group. It was . . . can you guess?

WRONG. It wasn't Gorkon—it was LAHN. He took a picture of Tatyana. (I suspected this all along, by the way.) Which made her smile and turn red, and then she grabbed the camera and took a picture of HIM. (I suspected THAT all along, too.) Then THEY disappeared.

Which was disturbing, as you might imagine, since—do the math—I was left alone with Gorkon. Who, as I watched Tatyana and Lahn fade off into the darkness of deck nine, jumped in front of me and snapped my picture. Then he handed me the camera.

Most uncomfortable situation, Delia. I felt bad about it, but I just COULD NOT take his picture. It wasn't because I was taking Gilligan's instructions too seriously or anything. It was because of FEAR. I was afraid that, given what the other Odd Squadians had done, he had gotten the idea that picture-taking was part of a human mating ritual, and that we would go off and make out once I got his photo. I was practically breaking out in hives at the thought.

"Gork," I said. "I like you—you're DIFFERENT."

He advanced toward me then (very much like R2-D2, I couldn't help but notice).

I stepped back, saying, "But it's a FRIEND thing. Like we'll miss each other after the trip, but we won't go around crying about it."

"Klingons don't have tear ducts," he said.

"See, there? THAT'S different—that's what I like about you," I said.

He stared at me (or my shirt, rather) for a VERY long minute or so and then said, "Aksh de ca lu tah." (Or something like that.)

"Huh?" I responded.

"You will be remembered with honor," he said.

Which was REALLY sweet, you must be thinking.

Or, since you are not nearly as nice a person as I obviously am, you may be thinking, "WHY IS SHE WASTING HER TIME WITH THIS LOSER WHEN THERE IS A EURO-HOTTIE TO FIND???" My answer to you: "I'm GETTING to that."

"Thanks, Gork," I said. "Maybe we could talk online sometime. Do you have a screen name?"

"KillKirk4591," he said.

"Okaaay," I said.

"Captain Kirk is the enemy of all Klingons," he explained.

"Okaaay," I repeated. "And is the '4591' your birthday?"

"No," he said. "I believe it means there are 4,590 other KillKirks."

Talking about his screen name made him want to get online, I guess, because he said he had some work to do in the Internet Café, and then he left. That's the last time I saw him. I hope I didn't hurt his feelings too much.

ANYWAY.

So, left completely alone, I began a very thorough exploration of the ship. The experience was very much like the treasure hunt, so I'll spare you the details and get to the point.

I'd been hunting for almost the whole hour and had come up with ZILCHO hotties—Euro or otherwise. I was getting ready to give up and call it a night, when, over my shoulder, I glimpsed HIM standing in the dining room. MY HOTTIE. And, oh YES, he was even EURO. I went in and talked to him, snapped his pic, and bounced (not literally—STOP laughing) back to the party and gave Gilligan the cam.

Fresh fruit smoothies were being made at the bar, so I got a strawberry one with a purple elephant perched on the rim of the glass. (I know now to steer clear of the monkeys.) More people were dancing than usual—and hugging each other and exchanging addresses and stuff—so I finally got a chance to play some foosball. There was a tournament going on (natch), and I made it three rounds before losing to the MAJOR gamer dude. (Who is from Austria, but is not anywhere near code-red. Yellow, at best.)

Then I plopped down in that same orange chair where I first saw AJ, and I spotted Tatyana and Lahn across the dance floor, looking happy. And then I saw Noori and AJ, and HE was crying now. (WHAT a sensitive guy—perhaps I should have given him more of a chance. Non.) Feeling left out of this love-a-thon happening in the teen lounge, I was ECSTATIC when Gilligan announced that the pictures were up.

We all flocked to the wall where he'd posted them and took a look at our ship's HOTTIES. Most of the shots were of kids standing there in the teen lounge, but some were of people from around the ship—the woman who runs the spa, the guy who stands at the door of the casino keeping kids out, some people who work at the shops, etc. Someone took a picture of Gilligan, which I was happy to see.

"Who is THAT?" we heard someone in the crowd ask, and then a bunch of people started laughing, because it was a picture of someone with no head—just a SHIRT. On the front were the words: Alexandria Recycles.

Crossing my arms over my chest and trying to look nonchalant, I wondered to myself: Is it possible Gorkon doesn't even realize I HAVE a head? Tatyana started cracking up, but I kicked her, and she shut up. (She responds to that sort of thing, since she is so much like you.)

"Where IS Gorky, anyway?" Noori asked, laughing, too. (I was so happy to be a source of such amusement.)

"Orbiting, I think," I said.

"Look at THAT," I heard someone else say, and then a whole new round of laughing started.

"Cristo?" Lahn said, laughing, too (very Frenchly).

"Who would take a picture of HIM?" AJ asked, laughing through his tears.

I felt GREAT that somehow I'd been able to return a favor to AJ. He'd dislodged a cherry from my throat, and I'd cheered him up. Because—yes, Delia—Cristo the hundred-year-old waiter was MY pick. OKAY, he's not what you had in mind for me, but I bet my grandmother would think he's hot.

The party ended shortly after that. Before it did, though, the five of us decided to do a fruit smoothie toast to our floating friendship. We went to the bar, and we each took a mango smoothie (to be ONE with each other), and we began our toasts.

"To Brady, who made it possible for me and AJ to get together!" Noori said, clanking her glass against mine. Which almost knocked off the yellow monkey that was dangling by its tail from the rim of her glass. (I decided not to tell her about the curse of the plastic monkeys.)

"To Tatyana," Lahn said, "who will come to Paris, I hope." (BOY, he'd SURE loosened up after getting hooked up.) (AND, by the way, his accent is WONDERFUL—very French.)

"To Noori!" AJ said, clanking his glass against hers, which made the monkey fall off completely. (Not sure what that means, curse-wise.) "Three months is too long," he added, choking up again.

"To my mother!" Tatyana said, clanking her glass against AJ's. "For agreeing to the fall trip."

"WHAT are we TALKING about?" I asked, toast-like, clanking my glass against Tatyana's.

"My mother said she'd take me and Noori to the USA!" Tatyana said.

"We'll be in DC, Brady," Noori said excitedly. "We can see you!"

"I can't wait to meet Delia," Tatyana said. "I can tell we have a lot in common."

(This is a new concern of mine, yes.)

"And it'll be when mah class is on a school trip to the nation's capital," AJ said, beaming.

"Wow!" I said, "WHAT a development. I am psyched!" And I clanked my glass against ALL of their glasses, which caused my own plastic glass thingie to fly off onto the floor.

But I picked it up. It's a blue mermaid. I have it in my pocket right now actually. I don't know why, but it feels like a good luck charm to me. I am hoping it will protect me from YOU when you go crazy on me for not finding a code-red Euro-hottie. Which encounter is going to happen in about a half hour, according to the pilot, who just made the announcement.

You want to know the truth, though, Delia? I don't CARE that I've failed with this particular THING. I know you think it's weird, but I guess boys just don't MATTER that much to me. Or, at least, any of the boys I've MET. But I am FINE with that. I am FINE with ME. THAT'S what this trip has given me, maybe—confidence! (Or, perhaps, the lucky mermaid is responsible.) I am ME, Delia. BRADY. THE BIG ONE. And it's—

Hold on a sec. The guy next to me has apparently awakened, and he's asking me something. (In a MOLTO BUONO Italiano accent.) He is saying:

"What sport do you play?"

"Huh?" I am saying back. (In my molto un-buono accent.)

"Is that not what 'jock' means?" he is asking, pointing to my palm, which I have unwittingly left out in the open on my little tray table.

"Mostly baseball," I say, moving my hand to a new position, where it hides both the writing AND this letter.

"I love baseball," he says. "I want to see a game in America—the Nationals!"

"I LOVE the Nationals," I say (wondering if that sounded stupid).

"You are also a geek?"

(Once again, thank you SO much, Delia. It has been such a pleasure to be known internationally as a geek.)

"It is good to be smart," he adds. "And did you find a code-red Euro-hottie?"

Okay. I guess he had a LOT of time to read my hand. I am VERY embarrassed. And, Delia, you know what? Now that I see this guy without his sleep mask, he is CUTE. I am feeling suddenly VERY tingly. Am I having a stroke or something? Or, do you think, Delia, that this is . . . he's EVEN wearing a blue shirt! That MUST be a sign! WHAT do I do NOW? HELP! HELP! HELP! I know! Maybe I should answer his question.

"DEFINITELY," I say.

"I am a high school exchange student from Firenza," he says. "I am, eh, staying with a family this year in a place called Old Town."

"That's, uh, exactly where I live." The cabin is spinning all of a sudden. Either I am about to faint, or the plane is crashing.

"They call it Old Town, but it is only two hundred years old?" he says. "In Italy, that would be a new town."

I just tried to laugh, but only a snort came out. I'm going to jump off this plane now.

"I am an art student. Do you know the National Gallery?"

"Definitely. I've been there lots. Awesome place."

"Maybe you could show me art there sometime."

(I am KEEPING that blue mermaid FOREVER.)

"Okay. I'm Brady."

"I am Guilio. Are those 'thrilling adventures' you are writing about?"

"Were. I'm all done, actually."

"Do you know, Brady, how I can get a bus from the airport?"

"We'll give you a ride. I'd like to introduce you to a friend."

(Is life a trip or WHAT?)

Brady

ABOUT THE AUTHOR

A child of the Washington, D.C. 'burbs, JANE HARRING-TON grew up with two brothers and three sisters, a mom and a dad, a beagle named Charlie, and a parakeet named Pudgie. Summers were spent submerged in the local swimming pool, and winter days waned in front of TV reruns of *Laugh-In* and *The Twilight Zone*. Despite many hardships (no computers, cell phones, DVDs, or microwave popcorn, to name just a few), she reached adulthood in the late 1970s. By 1990 she had three daughters, to whom she'd read aloud the entire collection of children's books at the local public library. That's when she started writing.

First published in *Spider* magazine, Jane went on to write fiction and nonfiction for a few other 'zines, then saw her first book—*Lucy's (Completely Cool and Totally True) E-Journal*—in print in the fall of 2001. *Four Things My Geeky-Jock-of-a-Best-Friend Must Do in Europe* is her first teen novel.

Today Jane lives in Alexandria, Virginia, with her cute and clever husband, Jon, and her incredibly inspiring daughters, Lucy, Emma, and Meghan (though she's in college most of the time). And—oh, yeah—her pets include a four-foot-long snake, a leopard gecko, a (totally weird) black cat, a ferret (who is adorable, but a huge mess), and sometimes a few giant hissing cockroaches and monarch butterflies. Jane loves to travel, hang out with her family, and watch the Washington Nationals play baseball.